His Daughter

Chloe Ricks

Contents

1

A N: Emmy Rossum as HaleyChapter 1

Haley sat on the couch as Tyson screamed at the sports game that was on TV. Every time he would scream she would flinch. He huffed and apologized again. Haley understood though. She didn't blame him, it wasn't his fault she would jump. She grew up with her dad, the next door neighbor Steven and his son Tyson screaming at the games every weekend. It just scared her now that the last thing she heard from her mother was a scream pleading for mercy.

Tyson was twenty and the next door neighbor that Haley lived her whole life with. Tyson was two years older than Haley but they were like brother and sister as they grew up next door with a close age range.

"We have some news!" Bethany, Tyson's mother bubbled and cheered coming through the door quickly also startling Haley but she quickly recovered.

"What is it?" Tyson asked as Haley nodded her head waiting for Bethany and her husband Steven to continue.

"We're moving to Colorado." The deep but soft voice of Steven spoke as he started entering the living room.

"Up by the mountains?" Tyson asked excitedly as he had previous knowledge of this.

The two nodded their head and Steven shot Haley a sad smile as she looked down to her lap.

Haley had a love hate relationship with Washington. It's were she grew up and had so much fun with her family and the minimal amount of friends she had but she was happy here. She spent her eighteen years of life here with her family.

Well more like seventeen years. That's why she hated Washington as well. About six months ago her parents were murdered in the same house she grew up in with her there. She stayed hidden in the attic for two days. Her mom told her to hide until the Devin's who were the family friends next door or police officers came looking for her. It just happened to take two days for them to come.

After her parents died is when she stopped talking.

She also stopped eating. So she really only slept or sat alone in the woods most the time. She just recently started hanging out with Tyson more just like she used too. By hanging out it's really just sitting by or with him as he does something, watches something, or talks.

"When do we leave?" Tyson asked his parents who always treated Haley like family. She was the daughter they never had. Especially since her parents passed.

"This Friday."

Steven walked to Haley and gently put his hand on her shoulder. Haley flinched not expecting the touch. She had only become jumpy after the incident. A delicate squeeze was given as she looked up.

"It will be okay. We will always take care of you." His quiet whisper reaches her ears as she had always had exquisite hearing and vision.

She merely nodded in response. She wasn't sure if she was sad that her only memories were here or if it was because if she left it would make her parents not being here with her so real.

She nodded and got off the couch walking to her room.

Bethany was about to walk after her to see what was wrong when Tyson stopped her.

"Give her some time then I'll go check on her." He reassured his mother.

Now it was about eight ten when the family started talking about the move. Topics like where they were moving, what it was gonna be like, who was already there, and what would Haley do came up in their conversations. They wrapped up around eight forty five.

While Steven and Bethany got ready for bed Tyson went up to Haley's room.

He softly knocked on the cream colored door and opened it a few seconds later when he heard no movement. He looked in to find Haley curled up into a tiny ball with her head on her pillow. Given her five foot two inch height and petite, weak frame, caused by not eating, added to the small size she was in comparison to the large queen bed.

"Hal?" He questioned softly.

She hardly moved her head to even look at him.

Tyson walked over to sit on the bed the way she was facing. He started to lightly rub her arm and push the hair stuck to her tear streaked cheeks out of her face.

"I know it's hard. This might be good though. You can get a change of scenery. There are nice woods up there. Meet new people. They have good colleges maybe you could go and start a career." Tyson offered with an optimistic view for Haley like he always tried to.

Haley curled into his side nodding her head as a soft sob left her lips. He waited till her breathing evened out and she fell asleep. Then he got up leaving the room.

Tyson was excited for Colorado. He would possibly find the girl he should mate with. He would have more power once he found her as well as getting the Alpha title just being there with a pack.

He hoped that Haley would find her mate. Tyson always had a soft spot for Haley. It was officially created when she was about five and fell into a bush. He helper he out, put a bandaid on her small cut, and she hugged him thanking him for everything like he saved her life. He always liked her before but that moment he knew he would protect her, look after her, care, and love her for the rest of their lives.

Tyson always knew at one point she would be happier, start to smile and laugh again. It broke a part of him to see basically his sister always sad and baring the loss of her parents.

Tyson had done everything for her. He tried to get her to eat again. He tried to get her to stop crying. He tried to get her to laugh or at least smile. And he tried to get her to talk again. His attempt of finally getting her to spend some time with him was now working. Yes she would just sit with him or something but at least she wasn't alone he always thought.

~

2

A N: Tyson

Chapter 2

Haley was woken up by the chatter down stairs. Her eyes were sore and stung as sunlight hit them. They were inevitably puffy and red from the crying she had done last night.

She changed out of the clothes that she wore yesterday and pulled up one of the very few pairs of yoga pants in her drawer. She grabbed a long sleeve shirt that used to fit her perfectly. Now it was loose and baggy on her deteriorating frame.

She pulled her wild and unruly black curls into a sloppy ponytail. She brushed her teeth and started splashing her hollowing face with water, she dried it and walked down stairs.

She was greeted by a hysterical Bethany running from kitchen to living room to kitchen. She was grabbing the throw blankets off the couch and then she would go into the kitchen. Seconds later she would come back out.

Haley paused the continuous loop that Bethany was on as she came to a stop realizing that Haley had woken up.

"There's breakfast in the kitchen honey." Beth smiled before she went back to her hectic day as Haley nodded in response.

She walked into the kitchen as Tyson shoveled food from his plate into his mouth. He looked up to smile with a mouth full of food greeting Haley. She nodded and noticed the bacon and hash browns on the table. Of course there was also eggs, pancakes, fruit, and other foods but Haley had always had a weakness to meats and potatoes. Meat was her all time favorite food. She could only eat in in small portions without throwing up now. But that was okay because as she ate one strip of bacon and two bites of hash browns she was already full.

That was caused by her lack of eating for two months and the minimal food she ate now. She believed she would be ignorant and dull-witted if she were to say she missed food when she missed her parents thousands of times more.

"Moms starting to pack. Would you like help with your stuff?" Tyson asked as he finished his plate.

Haley did the sign language motion for school. Tyson had made her learn simple words in sign language just so they could communicate easily without her having to write everything she wanted to say down. He nodded knowing it was Wednesday and she like to be punctual about everything.

"Today's the last day you'll be going. I'll still help you pack tonight or tomorrow if you want." Tyson replied getting ready to take Haley.

She was a senior in high school and was just looking to finish. She only took four classes and two were electives. She was always good in school getting all A's, taking advanced classes. This was the only year she took four classes and none were advanced. And it was all because she didn't want to do anything after her parents.

With some persuading from the Devin's they got her to stay in school instead of dropping out. She was partly thankful because she didn't stay in bed for the rest of her life doing nothing, even though she still thought this was a waist of her time.

She grabbed her back pack and walked out of the door and into the car. Tyson didn't talk until he was ready to drop her off.

"I'll pick you up after third if you want to get started on packing. Just let me know or I'll be here like usual. Mom took care of everything for moving so don't worry."

She nodded and got out of the car. Walking into school she was basically invisible. She had no friends now that she had shut everybody out and no one wanted to bother reading her reply after they asked her something.

She wasn't bullied for not talking or not dating which most of the school did. Everyone had there own little clique and was super close.

The weird things that Haley noticed about people is how their eye color changes. Everyone has their own color when their mad. When they are looking at their boyfriend or girlfriend usually they turn dark or black. It happened to most people so she just ignored it.

She went through her first two classes learning nothing, doing nothing, and bored out of her mind. She decided a start on packing wouldn't be bad. She texted Tyson asking if he could pick her up after third. He quickly replied yes.

While Haley sat there bored as Tyson was in his fathers office talking about the land they would gain in the move. They would run a small pack and live on the outskirts of the city that has a small population of one hundred and twenty seven. It was about a total of thirty families. They were all werewolves and everyone knew everyone. He would be bordering with one of the most feared Alphas in the world. That only caused him a little glint of fear when he thought about Haley.

She loved the woods and was always drawn to it. She always wanted to explore even if she was told not to go to far in. That's what scared him. What if she walked to far into the woods crossing territory lines. Would they immediately kill her thinking she was a rouge?

He shook the thought as he got a text from Haley. He had about forty five minutes till he should go pick her up and he was done talking to his father. Not waisting time he went into his room and started to pack up things that he wouldn't need till they got to the new house and clothes he wouldn't wear till after the move ether.

Shortly later he left to pick Haley up and bring her home. He asked when she wanted to pack but she just shrugged her shoulders. She didn't really care and she didn't really want to. It's not that she felt one way or another about the move. It's just that she felt blah. She didn't really care. She started to feel numb again.

He nodded kissing her forehead as she turned into her room. She discarded the unneeded bra that was not useful as she had nothing much to fill it in. She crawled into bed to fall asleep, her body exhausted from the little she had done today.

~AN: Please vote and comment! Have a wonderful read!

3

C hapter 3

All of Thursday Haley had puttered around the house or her room with Tyson. He helped her or really did it by himself in getting down suitcases and they did a little bit of everything. Tyson had already packed up his room and was going through Haley's to see if she wanted to bring everything in it or just some stuff.

'Are we driving?' Haley wrote down on her pad of paper she had in her room.

"Yeah it will be about thirteen hours, give or take a few. Dad wants to drive the whole way." Tyson answered letting her know partly how they would go about getting to their new home.

Haley nodded knowing she would want and need a pad of paper, a pen, and a blanket in the car with her.

At dinner Steven gave everyone the plan for tomorrow.

They would pack everything needed into the car tonight the rest would be picked up by a friend and sent over. They would be leaving the house at three o'clock in the morning. Around seven or eight they would most likely drive through for breakfast and take a bathroom stop. They had snacks that Bethany had already packed in the car for lunch and would take a bathroom break as needed. With the hopes to arrive by about three or four but with the time change it will really be about five o'clock there.

Depending on what they felt like by the time they got there they would ether unload a few things, all things or just go to bed. The house was bought semi furnished so they had beds and couches already there for them.

Haley just nod to the plan not really caring how they got there, in what time frame or what order. All she knew is they were going to White River and that they were going to basically be surrounded by pure, luscious, green forest.

Haley helped clean and then box the rest of the silverware that they had used for dinner with Bethany. Steven and Tyson were loading the big car with as much stuff as they could possibly fit. The hardest part was fitting in the rest of Bethany's clothes. Both of the men had two suitcases and two other bags. Haley only had one suitcase and two bags where as Bethany had Three suitcases and three bags.

Tyson cursed as a high heel stabbed his hand through the bag. He was so frustrated that he just threw the bag in closing the back hatch.

All of the appliances and furniture would be sold with the house making Haley's room look clean but dull. Walking up the stairs Haley only had blank walls, a chest for her clothes, and the bed. The bed held the blanket she would bring with them tomorrow and the clothes that she would throw on in the morning. She was now in pajamas that she could easily put in the car or slide in a bag.

Her thick heavy curls began to start bothering her as she started to get a headache. She felt like she could feel every single follicle of hair as everything from the very short week had built up.

She walked to find Bethany changing into her night wear. Beth smiled as Haley walked in. She held up a hair tie which was her way of asking the question.

"Braided my darling?" Bethany asked as Haley nodded sitting on the edge of the bed.

Bethany started the braid with Haley's unkept and unruly curls that were more like waves at times. Admiring the shoulder length dark brown hair with natural highlights of a lighter brown shade running through few strands.

"Does it hurt?" She asked gently pulling more hair into the braid. Bethany knew that Haley had a headache and was asking about it. A nod came from Haley.

Bethany had a weird instinct on knowing everything that could be wrong and would be wrong and is wrong with Tyson and Haley. It was like a mom instinct. She knew Haley liked her hair braided when she was getting or had a headache. She also seemed to know what causes her headache, when, and what would help relieve or get completely rid of it.

Bethany massaged Haley briefly once she had finished the braid. At the top of her neck and base of her skull she applied pressure releasing tension from her head and back. Now relaxed Haley started to feel more tired and sleepy. She signed goodnight to Bethany and walked into the room of nothing cuddling into the blanket she got from her parents on her tenth Christmas.

They were out shopping together and Haley saw it in a baby store. She felt it and instantly fell in love. It had reminded her of a baby blanket she had when she was young. One side was silk that she would rub on her face at night while falling asleep and the other side was Cotton, but this blanket was more extravagant and finely detailed as well as much bigger being the size of an actual blanket instead of a baby blanket. Her parents told her that they were a little tight on money as it was the Christmas season. Haley understood after she looked at the price of a hundred dollars. In her young mind that was more than expensive. She dismissed the thoughts of having the blanket without a complaint and moved on.

That Christmas morning the exact blanket with a cream silk trim and a tan fuzzy sides was a Christmas present. She forever loved it and always slept with it. At this point she couldn't get to sleep without it unless she was that tired. The light touch of silk against her skin pulled her into a soft warm sleep.

~AN: I hope you enjoy this book and keep reading!

I love you my beautiful people!

Please vote and comment my chickens

4

C hapter 4

So it was two fifty in the morning when Steven went around pounding on all the bedroom doors startling Tyson from his sleep as he jumped from his peaceful sleep falling out of the bed onto the floor as he was at the edge of the bed to begin with. Steven then walked to Haley's room opening it up and shaking her awake.

When Steven made a plan he really likes to stick to it. It was almost three and they were not in the car.

Tyson realized this and stated to rush. He hated when his dad yelled at him and even more when it was because he didn't stick to a stupid plan that his father thought was so important.

Tyson then realized that Haley had never been through a plan rage, by his father, as he likes to call it. This made him hurry to pull on his shirt as he started running into Haley's room. She had finished pulling up her pants as he barged right in. She only had a thin camisole on as her sleeping shirt but her breasts had shrunk with the weight loss so there wasn't much to see and if anything Tyson was the only boy to see anything of hers.

"Pick up your shoes we have to get in the car before dad starts yelling!" Tyson rushed out grabbing the jacket she was going to wear and he picked up the flannel pajama shorts she had next to it.

After she picked up her shoes barely grabbing her blanket she was thrown over the shoulder of Tyson. He ran down the stairs as his father opened the front door. He got in to the car pulling Haley from his should into his lap.

"Oh I'm sorry I didn't want us to get yelled at." He spoke breathlessly as he hugged her.

She nodded and Tyson helped her over to the passenger side of the car.

"Hopefully mom gets here in time so you don't have to experience dads rage." Haley nodded again but this time with a purpose.

She was still half asleep and wanted to go back to sleep. Yelling was never on her list of things to hear especially now that it was almost three in the morning and she was tired.

Bethany got in the passenger seat with her purse and a bag of anything important left through the house along with snacks for the road.

Steven got in the car and started it up. It was two fifty nine, just saving the three from getting yelled at over a minute. Haley sat there staring at the next door house silently saying her goodbyes and I love yous in her head.

By the time Steven pulled out of the driveway Tyson was leaning against the door with one leg up on Haley's lap and she was also leaning on the door wrapped up in her blanket.

The two in the back drifted to sleep before the streets turned into freeway. Bethany was in and out of a light sleep as this was really early for her but she wanted to stay up to make sure her husband was okay to drive, knew where to go, and was aware of his surroundings with the early time.

Hours later she looked to the backseat. Spread across the back seat was her six foot son who's head was now laying in the curled up lap of Haley. Haley had stayed in almost the exact same position except for the angle of her head and the way her lap was positioned now with Tyson's big head on it. Beth smiled at the two. They were always good friends when they were little and then they got super close as brother and sister. Where Haley was Tyson was and where Tyson was Haley was. It's just how the two were growing up. After Haley stop talking and started to isolate herself Tyson was really the only one that she was around longer than thirty minutes at a time. Bethany was the next person she would spend the most time with. She always thought it was because she had always seen her as an aunt and would come to her if she needed something, like Christmas gifts for her parents.

Bethany missed Hadlee and Jake. They were always like family spending time together and helping one another. They always protected each other and took responsibility for each other's children when the other couldn't. They had promised each other that if anything ever happened they would keep the others child safe and cared for.

That's a small part of why they're moving, as well as Tyson becoming Alpha and running a pack.

Haley's parents weren't just killed by a thief who didn't want caught. It was all planed out. And according to the note they had found before finding Haley, she was their next target. She just never needed to know that. Steven and Tyson could never even figure out who 'they' were as well so they didn't know who to look out for.

The two families weren't in a pack now besides the Alpha work from afar that Steven did and both had left loving packs filled with their families so that was out of the running. For goodness sakes Haley didn't even know werewolves were a thing. Let alone that she and all the people around her were one.

No one understood why Haley didn't shift and she never thought anything of it as she was raised in a civilized town with some humans. Wolves couldn't just go running around whenever they wanted and her parents didn't know how to tell her.

Haley had woke up to eat and to pee. Bethany and Tyson had switched spots so she could nap before they arrived. They only had about an hour or so left to go before they arrived at the house. The whole family had stayed awake for the last two hours of the trip as they soon pulled into the street with three big houses spaced out facing a line of forest trees. Steven pulled into the last driveway and shut off the car.

Haley took in the plush forest green grass the covered the whole yard until it meet a brick walkway heading to a bright red door covered by a porch. The whole house was a very light gray with a tint of brown and the trimming around the roof, windows, and door frame was a white making the house look clean.

~Hope you have a safe Memorial Day and take a minute to thank the fallen for our lives and freedom.

Have a great day cuties! Please vote and comment

5

C hapter 5

Bethany adored the giant house that was bigger than necessary and much more homey than expected for the large size of it. Walking into the house it was definitely way more than just semi furnished. This house was fully furnished with the three couches in the living room and a TV to go with them.

A dinning room table that seats six. The refrigerator, dishwasher, microwave, oven, and stove were all there in a 'slate' stainless steel. The kitchen was rustic but very modern. There was beautiful wood in any place it should be but there was also the steel and light still flowing in making it look big and more open even with the island taking up room.

Connected to the kitchen there was beautiful French doors that led to a big open backyard. There was a small garden already started and a tab bit further it started the forest line.

This pulled Haley to the backdoor. She was lost in her thought of how alluring the giant wood trunks and once vibrant green leaves change colors with the seasons and fell to the dark dirt.

"Later." Steven spoke tenderly placing his big hand over her shoulder blade.

He pulled Haley from her thoughts and nodded. Not only did he not want her to go out alone like he did ever since she moved in with them but he was also telling her that they should get in and settled before exploring around.

Haley turned from the back doors and walked out to the car. Tyson was pulling out her bags as well as his. Anything left in the car was picked up and she picked up a bag before Tyson led her back into the house. She followed him up stairs and he stopped between two rooms.

"You can pick the one you want. I'll take the other." He spoke opening the door he was next to. It was a very big room with a walk in closet, king size bed, desk, adjoining bathroom, a love seat facing a big flat screen TV, and a enormous chest for all his clothes. The color theme in the room was a navy blue, gray, and white.

She nodded knowing what was in that room and then walked across the hall to see what was in the other room and what it looked like.

As she opened the door you could tell that it was noticeably smaller. There was a full bed, a regular closet, a small chest for clothes that are not on hangers, a night stand next to the bed, and a window seat where the whole window actually opens to the right and folds neatly against the wall. There was no flat screen, bathroom, or couch but that didn't mater to Haley.

She turned to Tyson and pointed down signaling she wanted this one. A confused look crossed his face and he nodded his head.

"But why?" He asked to curiously not to.

She pointed to the window and then she signed the letters for him to completely understand.

"Oh. You wanted to see the forest." He realized now understanding.

She nodded her head and slowly walked over to hug him. She silently thanked him for giving her the option to choose even if he didn't get what he wanted. He just wanted her to be happy.

"Let's get all your stuff in and unpacked. Okay?" He asked pulling the suitcase and bags to the bed.

She agreed as Tyson stated to take out the clothes that already had hangers on them. Haley started to fill the chest with folded clothes. She really only needed two drawers but it had three so she spaced the little clothes she had out neatly.

She took out her only decoration being her favorite color of brown on the picture frame and a picture of her mom, dad, and her. It matched the room that was painted a light cream with light gray baseboards around the room. The bed sheets were white and the bed spread was a darker gray. There wasn't much other color to it but that was okay with her.

"I believe we're going out for dinner in an hour, so if you want to change you can go ahead. I'll be in my room if you need anything." Tyson said walking out.

Haley wasn't very hungry. She was unsure if it was because of the move and the new change which she never liked change to begin with or if it was just she wasn't hungry.

She didn't change because there was no point in changing from what she had on to something exactly like that for she had no extravagant clothes. When Tyson came she followed him to the car where Bethany and Steven had just walked out to. They got in the car and started driving. She wasn't sure where they went or what she even got because she was only going to have a few bites of whatever it was.

While they were waiting they were talking about what they liked about the house, their room, or the city in general. Haley signed very little to Tyson who spoke for her because she didn't have a pen to write it out for the adults.

Bethany told Haley everything for school. She was going to start on Monday and she only had three classes now. One of the elective classes was not offered here and she didn't need a certain number of classes to take as long as she was eighteen. Bethany also offered to take her out shopping so she had new clothes for school but Haley declined. Bethany didn't just want new clothes but she wanted to buy nicer clothes as Haley only sported oversized shirts and jackets with jeans or leggings.

After the dinner they went back to the house now called home. The couple went to finish unpacking. Tyson went to watch TV and rest. Haley went to take a shower in the bathroom next to her room. After that she went to her room holding her blanket with one final look at her picture. Then she was asleep.

~AN: OMG IM TERRIBLE! I completely forgot to post yesterday. Ugh! I'm just ready to graduate.

I'm sorry my loves.

Please vote and comment.

6

C hapter 6

The weekend went by extremely fast as they finished or at least tried there best to finish getting the house ready for everyday living and just like it used to be.

Bethany and Haley didn't go shopping as Haley denied the variety of pleas that Bethany tried. Haley didn't want nor did she think she needed new clothes besides she really didn't want to go out anywhere other than the backyard or forest as that is what it really is. The change of scenery only made her miss her parents more. This was exhaustingly emotional and along with her malnourished health it made her very tired.

Haley had slept for a plethora of more hours than she was awake. Tyson talked to her very little after Friday night in fact he only talked very slightly when they went to the backyard to explore for the first time.

Tyson was preparing for his new role and job here. He was definitely not trying to ignore his mother and Haley. In fact every time when Haley missed a meal that the rest ate he always went up to check on her. It just so happened that every time she was sleeping.

Monday morning came with alarms that ranged from five to seven in the morning. First up was Steven as it was his usual to wake up so early. Next was Tyson who woke up preparing for introductions as alpha tonight and everything else that came with the job. Bethany was the next up as she liked to make breakfast for everyone. She no longer had to wake up early as well because she no longer had or needed a job. Finally the last to wake up was Haley.

She was not the least bit thrilled this Monday morning. Not only did she have to wake up early but she had to go out into public with people for a longer amount of time than she thought necessary which happened to be a little over three hours and thirty minutes.

Nevertheless she got up finding pants and a long sleeve as it was slightly chilly out. She pulled on socks and shoes, walking down stairs. She walked into the kitchen only to see Steven leaving and Bethany doing dishes.

"Here honey. I know your not hungry but you need something before you go." Bethany said pushing two slices of apple and a piece of bacon over to her.

Haley excepted her offer knowing it was in her best interest as she already was slowly forming a headache.

'Tyson?' Haley wrote asking where he was.

"He's taking care of some business. I will be taking you to school when you're ready." Bethany answered.

Haley pointed to the ground indicating that she was ready to go now.

Bethany grabbed her purse and keys and Haley grabbed her backpack. They walked out the door into the car that was delivered over the weekend. Bethany drove quietly and when she got there she let Haley know that she will pick her up on the corner after her last class.

Haley nodded walking in. She was searching for the office to pick up her schedule as people stared at her oddly. She finally found the door and walked in.

Teachers and adults bustled around as they started their day. Haley walked up to a desk with an older woman behind it. The woman looked up and smiled cheerfully. Haley only nodded in return.

"What can I help you with?" She bubbled over as if it was an exciting conversation.

Haley searched her pocket for her pen once she found her paper. Once she dug it out of her pocket she started to write.

'I'm new here. My name is Haley.' She pushes it towards the women who looked at her in fascination.

She read the note before nodding.

"This is your schedule. You only have three classes. The elective we picked is a teachers assistant for your third class. It's the same teacher as your first class." The older women spoke pointing to the different parts of the schedule.

She also showed Haley where the classes were and how to read the schedule.

Haley signed 'thank you' as it was quite common for most to know. As she walked out the bell had rang and the halls were completely empty. She scavenged through the halls in search for the class. Once she found it she walked in interrupting the class lesson. Everyone's gaze was instantly on her.

"Who are you?" The teacher asked curiously.

Haley had the paper and pen in hand. She walked closer and started writing.

'Haley. I'm new.'

"Well miss Haley. Will you find your seat so I can get back to class?"

She nodded to the man and quickly found an open spot till someone moved a bag there. She kept walking till she was at the back. All the kids seemed to stare at her as if she was some freak. But that was to be expected as she didn't speak and transferred into the school close to the end of the semester.

The same thing happened in her second class because she had trouble finding it. That was not the case for her third and final class though. She got there on time and wrote to the teacher why she was back. She sat to the side of class ignoring everything till the bell rang.

Bethany was there as promised. She got in and they drove home. Haley decided time out in the woods would be best. So that's where she went till the end of the day. Bethany, Steven, and Tyson all left that evening, leaving Haley alone. She didn't care. It just gave her time for a long uninterrupted bath as she stared into the woods while thinking making her somewhat emotional and then she went to bed.

~ AN: because I screwed up last week and this week is busy but I'm free today here you go!

Hopefully I can update on Wednesday as well.

Have a great week!

Please vote and comment my loves

7

C hapter 7

This same routine happened every day with the exception of weekends. The only difference was they were all there every night besides Wednesday's. On Wednesday they all go to pack meetings with the people higher up in the pack. All but Haley who still had no clue werewolf's were a real thing that wasn't made up.

School was very boring for Haley. The academic classes that she did take were multiple chapters behind on the lessons or the class read the book in the opposite order that she had original done in Washington making her have already known, read, and wrote about the books she was supposed to be reading in class.

When she had work she would usual do it during her third class as the teacher had no work for her to do anyways.

Many of the kids would still give her weird looks or whisper about her when she would walk by in the halls. No one knew she could hear everything they were saying.

Some oddly talked about the way she smelt. Few talked about where she's from or where she lives now. Some came up with gossip about why she didn't talk. She didn't care what they said. None of it was right and no one asked her so it didn't really matter. She did kind of wish that they would keep it to themselves or wait till she's actually out of hearing distance. She was glad that most kids did go on their way and didn't really care that she was here.

Haley used to be invisible and she realized she liked it much better just from the month she had been here and had few kids talk about her.

She took a deep breath letting it out slowly as she waiting for the bell to ring. She followed behind the rush of students heading out of class when it did ring. She walked past the corner remembering that Bethany was not going to pick her up because she was busy as well as Tyson and Steven.

Tyson did throw a small fit when he found out she was going to be walking home by herself. It's not that he thought she couldn't but he didn't want her to and he wanted her safe like the older over protective brother he is. With the title of Alpha he did become more possessive over his family as well though.

Tyson was sitting in a meeting with a few other Alphas talking about how they wanted to throw a big fancy party for the new Alpha. He was secretly waiting for his phone to buzz with a message from Haley saying she got home okay. But he was to eager as at this time Haley had only made it halfway on the little bit under a half mile walk home.

Tyson was so caught up waiting for the text that he missed most of the people they would be inviting. It really didn't matter to him anyways. Soon his phone buzzed and a smile slid across his face.

"Alpha Tyson?" He was pulled from his thoughts as he looked up. "Is he okay to invite?" The man asked.

"Oh yes. Sorry." He apologized for not paying attention but then he realized he didn't know who he approved on coming. It didn't matter as long as he knew Haley was safe right now.

Haley had taken a nap and was now walking through the woods. This was farther than she had gone before and it was darker but it also seemed brighter as the vivid colors stuck out against dark and nude tones. She breathed in the fresh scent enjoy and the susurrus around her.

She decided to head back just as the three came home from their busy life's and they talked about it in the kitchen.

Well all except Haley talked. She just listened taking everything in.

Tyson lastly announced that he was having a party for becoming alpha.

"A few of the people I work with are throwing a big party on Friday." He spoke making sure his parents knew it was the other Alphas and making sure Haley still didn't know about werewolf's.

This caused a roar of excitement from Bethany who loved parties and dressing up fancy. She jumped and clapped and cheered as her husband stare at her in awe. He loved this excited side of his wife and thought it was beautiful they way her smile expanded and radiated off her onto him.

After she settled a little she started dinner. They were all talking about the party as they ate.

"Your coming right?" Tyson asked Haley with pleading eyes.

She just kinda shrugs and lightly shook her head no. A sad frown came over Tyson's face as she shook her head.

"Please? I really want you there. It's not like you have to meet anyone. Just go for me." He pleaded with his sad face.

With a heavy breath she nodded as Tyson's pearly white smile spread across his face. Haley always hated to disappoint Tyson so she would go to his party to make him happy.

"Oh good! I know you don't like shopping so I'll go get you a beautiful dress and help you get ready. How about that?" Bethany cheered again.

Haley was the girl Beth never had so it always made her happy. Haley just nodded wanting to please the family in front of her.

After dinner Haley helped Bethany clean up as the two men went to talk in the office. As they were cleaning and putting stuff away Bethany continued talking about the dress and what style she thought it should be and how it looked or was designed. She went on to talk about the different styles they could do with her hair and the jewelry with different dresses along with makeup.

That's when Haley stopped. She was never one for much make up. She never owned it, had the need to use it, or every really wanted to use it. She enjoyed looking at all the different colors that people use and what they can do with it but she never found a personal interest for makeup on her. So she immediately shook her head no hopping she wouldn't have to wear a lot if any.

"Oh it's okay dear we won't do a lot just a little mascara and some lipstick. It will be like nothings even on." Bethany reassured as Haley threw a skeptical nod.

~~~~~~~~~~~~~~~~~~~~~~~~~~~~ Susurrus- low soft sound, a quite wind or a rustling

~AN: chapter up!!!

I'm so tired but it doesn't even mater I can fail all my finals and it doesn't matter
~~~~~~~~~~~~~~~~~~~~~~~~~~~~

One more day of school!!!

Anyways!!! Please vote and comment my loves!

8

C hapter 8

Friday came much quicker than expected for Haley. She wasn't sure if she was ready to be spending hours in a room with so many people. She wasn't even sure if she was ready to wear a dress.

Friday didn't seem to come fast enough for Bethany. She had found the exact same dress that she had made up in her mind for Haley. It was much more revealing than what Haley was used to but she thought it would go perfect with her frail body shape.

Haley walked home on Friday because she liked the slight walk and smell of the woods. She somehow convinced Tyson to let her walk. Really she said she needed to be alone before thrown into a room with a bunch of people which Tyson understood and obliged.

She got home texting Tyson and going out in the woods for an hour. She needed to be outside and alone before the party tonight. That's really the only way she would be able to function with so many people around.

Once she came back inside Bethany asked her to eat something before she showered. Bethany knew that Haley would most likely not be eating at this party and she always worried about her health after her parents death. Haley agreed and ate half of the sweet green kiwi that was offered to her.

"Go take a shower while I get ready. Once I'm done I'll come help you." Bethany spoke pushing her up the stairs.

Bethany slipped into her black gown that fell widely around her hips and was tight on her bust. She grabbed her emerald colored earrings and bracelet. For makeup she had a nude smokey eye with a pink lipstick. She pulled her reddish brown color hair into a sleek low bun with a part down the middle. Once she was satisfied she changed her purse into a smaller clutch as she just heard the bathroom shower turn off.

Haley took longer than usual in the shower as she was unsure of what she was wearing and where to shave. She shaved everything in the event that Bethany would give her something releasing to wear. She got out of the shower towel drying her hair and then her body. She wrapped a towel around her hair and one around her body as she walk into her room. Bethany was bringing in her dress with a big smile.

"So let me do your hair and makeup and we can get your dress on." Bethany explained as Haley nodded not having a preference on what they did.

Haley sat on the toilet facing the wall while Bethany was blowing her hair dry. They waited for the straightener to heat up and Bethany decided to start her make up.

She put a very light layer of powder on to even out any discoloration on the blemish free face. She grabbed the eyeliner and did a line across while only going one fourth of the way towards the inside of her eye on the bottom lash line. She then applied a coat of mascara and a light nude lipstick.

Going back to her hair she parted it down the middle and started to straighten. Once straight she ran back through it doing loose curls to each piece. Once satisfied Bethany pulled Haley into her room she told her to close her eyes as she put on the dress. Haley followed directions closing her eyes and stepping into the dress. Once it was zipped up Bethany turned her and she opened her eyes.

The long black dress plunged at her chest. There was a gold wavy line over her hip that connected to the slit going up to her mid thigh.

Haley started at herself in shock how her small body filled out this dress and how her face was more lively than before.

"I know you can wear and walk in heels so I got you some as well." Bethany smirked looking into the mirror at her beautiful daughter she never had.

Haley sat on the bed and with the help of Bethany strapped up the black heels that had two straps over her toes and two holding the shoe to her ankle.

She stood up and they gave her a nice three inch lift.

She signed thank you and hugged Bethany as she smiled brightly. A honk brought them out of the hug.

"Okay let's go. They're waiting for us." Bethany grabbed her clutch and excitedly bounced down the stairs.

Once outside Steven and Tyson were waiting outside the car. Tyson mouth dropped open as he saw his little sister walking out of the house. He had never seen her look so gorgeous and grown up. Stevens face beamed with a smile at his happy wife and beautiful daughter.

"You look lovely lady's." Steven spoke as he took Bethany's hand. She blushed lightly still loving her husbands complements. Haley gave a slim tight line smile in response as appreciation.

Tyson helped Haley in the car as his father did the same for his mother. Once they started to dive Tyson leaned over to Haley.

"You look stunning Hal. Thank you for coming. It really means a lot." He gently squeezed her hand.

Haley nodded looking at him and gave him a kiss on the cheek an action that she hadn't preformed in a while.

Tyson smiled as he knew that was something she would always do before what happened with her parents. He slightly saw the old Haley come back and he enjoyed it immensely.

Steven pulled into a giant gated mansion with a Victorian area look to it that Haley enjoyed to look at. There were shrubs that grew up to the steps of the beige color home. There was luscious green grass ran on both sides of the gravel semi circle drive. There was a huge fountain in the grass by the front gate.

Steven parked the car right in line with the row. Both men got out and opened the door for the two ladies.

Haley immediately clung to Tyson with a slight look of fear. It was partly because she was wearing high heels which she hadn't in a long time and was attempting to walk on gravel. The other part that was the much bigger reason, because there were so many cars and she already saw people smiling and greeting each other.

~AN: I'm so happy my laptop came! I'm just happy in general so DOUBLE UPDATE!

Vote and comment cuties!

9

C hapter 9

A part of why Haley held fear in her expression was because there were so many cars and she already saw people smiling and greeting each other.

"It's okay. Once we get inside you can pick where you'd like to sit and you can ignore everyone the rest of the night." Haley nodded to Tyson.

At the steps a few people had greeted them and Tyson kindly said hello. Once inside Haley was already on the search for a unoccupied table in a dark corner with no one around. And she found the perfect one. She tapped Tyson lightly and pointed over to the left side of the room away from everything.

They all walked to the table and Haley sat down.

"Are you sure you want to stay here by yourself?" Bethany asked with a sad face.

Haley nodded giving a reassuring look to all three of them.

"Okay. I'll be over there if you need me." Bethany pointed over by the bar and dance floor. She nodded understandingly.

Tyson was the last to leave as Bethany pulled Steven with her over to the bar to mingle and socialize with people.

"I'll be all around but I'll keep an eye on you. If you need something just wave my down." He spoke before kissing the top of her head and leaving.

About an hour had passed and Haley had positioned herself perfectly. She had a full view of the room and she could see the top of the stair case where everyone entered in.

Many more people had came and the right side of the huge ball room was filled while the left side had couples chatting at tables spread around the room.

Haley had only gotten a few odd looks as she was sitting in the corner alone. But that was to be expected at an event like this. No one has tried to come up to talk to her and she was thankful for that.

Every man and woman in here were beautiful. The women were slim and curvy while being tall and well put together. The men were like giants compared to Haley even in the heals and they had bulging muscles through the suits they wore. Less than more of the men had a well defined face but all were handsome just the same.

Peoples were buzzing around, eating, talking, laughing, some even getting drunk but most were just tipsy if anything.

Tyson had been going around meeting family's from his pack and the packs of his allies. He smelt the delectable scent of blueberries and what seemed to be a fresh poppyseed muffin. He followed that to find a tall blonde in a beautiful white dress. There eyes met and he whispered the word that the nameless girl longed to hear.

"Mate."

Tyson strides over to her quickly as she stood there frozen taking her mate in. He stood tall in front and then he swooped down pressing his lips to hers as he cup her cheek. Sparks shot through them as warmth and love ran through their bodies, hearts, and minds. They pulled apart breathlessly when they finally spoke.

"I'm Tyson. What your name my wonderful mate."

"I'm Natal- You're my new Alpha." She cut herself off short as shock ran threw her with the realization.

"No I'm just your mate my sweet Luna." He whispered softly kissing her lips.

"I'm Natalie." She spoke with a breathtaking smile.

*

Haley looked around finding Bethany and Steven dancing together. The way Steven looked at his wife with so much love and the way she looked back at him made Haley's heart clinch at the memories of her parents. Most the of the people that had a date actually reminded her of her parents.

They loved each other so much. Her father would always find a way to tell Haley's mother that he loved her more. With a frustrated and emotional huff Hayley was pulled out of her thoughts as the doors at the top of the grand staircase bursted open.

Everyone in the room froze. After a few seconds some whispers spread around the room. The man at the top of the stairs let out a low growl and everyone returned to what they were doing. Except Haley.

She stared at the man at the top of the stair case with his nose in the air as if he was trying to pick up a certain scent as if he was trying to find cookies in a home without knowing where the kitchen was. The man was in a dark gray suite with a black shirt underneath. The suit jacket was unbuttoned but was snug on his bulging arms and the pants were tight on his giant thighs. His black shoes matched his belt as well. He had flawless bronzed skin popping out of the three top buttons of his wrinkle free shirt. The thick stump like neck led up to sharp jaw bone and a square chin. He had a pointed nose, full heart shaped lips, beautiful brown eyes that shine in the light of the chandelier, and dark chocolate hair that shines with a healthy glow. She noticed he had a lot light stubble on his chin growing in as he continued to look around.

Pulled from her thoughts Bethany, Steven, and Tyson ran up to the table with a gorgeous blonde next to Tyson.

"Love, how are you?" Bethany asked with urgency and worry.

Haley nodded her head that she was okay and they all relaxed a little but were still kinda stiff.

"It's getting late. Maybe we should get home." Steven said as she just nodded and they picked everything up.

Walking to the door, Steven put his hand on the handle and they heard a loud menacing growl. It startled Haley so she turned around to see the handsome man who barged into the room just recently storming their way, but everyone else froze.

"Okay let's go." Steven said as he was the first to recover from his shock.

He pulled Haley's arm out of the door quickly walking causing her to stayed at a light jog to keep up. They were in the car with the unfamiliar blonde. Haley looked over to the doorway seeing the man standing there.

Haley was confused about the whole thing but really about the girl in the car. So she tapped Tyson's arm and pointed at her.

"This is my girlfriend Natalie." She looked over and said hi with a smile after Tyson's reply. Looking up Haley nodded her head in approval.

They were soon home and everyone relaxed visibly. Haley went up to her room undressed and fell asleep quickly as just being in the same room as all those people made her tired.

~ AN: last day of class!!!! I'm pumped for California adventure tomorrow!!!

New chapter for my excitement!

Vote and comment my lovelies!

10

C hapter 10

Xavier was extremely pissed. He finally got to look at his mate and she was ripped right from his sight.

The faint scent of something floral with the fresh and clean scent of lemon came to his nose as he first barged past the doors and into the room. It was faint and he couldn't pick up the trail to follow it but he knew he wanted almost needed too. He had continued to walk in to find the scent and who it was coming from. He was to stunned to speak when it rushed right past him as the family of five quickly climbing the stairs.

A low growl ripped through his chest as his mate tried to escape. Everyone froze as well as her but she had looked over her shoulder finding Xavier's intense stare on her. Steven the man holding her arm said something and pulled her to the car. Haley had to stay at a light jog to keep up with the quick pace they were walking at.

They all got in the car and drove away. Xavier was furious but somewhat thankful that he now only had to play the waiting game.

Haley had fallen asleep after she changed. Tyson's parents met his mate and talked slightly before all going to bed. Tyson pulled his mate into his chest and sighed contently.

"Why did we leave the party so quickly with Harley? No wait Haley, right?" She questioned thoughtful looking up to him after she corrected her mistake of the similar names.

"Haley doesn't know she's a wolf. She doesn't even know we're wolfs. With Alpha Daron sniffing around like that we didn't want to take any chances of the most ruthless Alpha possibly being her mate. He would take her and throw her into a world she's not used to causing her to break any progress she had made so far. But with the way he stormed after us I'm guessing he'll be here to take her soon." Tyson sighed wishing only the best for Haley.

"Why doesn't she talk? What happened?" She asked with concern for Tyson's loved one in her eyes.

"Her parents were killed basically in front of her and she hid in the attic for two days till we found her." The mood turned somber if it wasn't already.

"Oh that's terrible. That poor thing." Natalie said as her heart ached for Haley just like a Luna should for her pack members.

"It's okay love. She's been getting better. We just have to keep supporting her." Natalie nodded to Tyson's statement as he turned off the last light in the house and fell asleep.

Xavier had waited an hour more just for good measures before he did anything. He came out of the woods behind the Devin residence looking up at the three windows. He followed the scent of flowers and lemon to the two windows on the right side of the house. Taking a closer look he realized one window was bigger and opened with a bench seat there as well. He figured that would be her room.

Haley dreamed of a soft breeze blowing threw her window as she sat at the window seat. The moon was a crescent hovering above the tall trees. A howl of a wolf caught her ear. She looked down in the forest hopping to spot just a glimpse of the beautiful creatures. She froze as a colossus black wolf chasing after a much smaller light brown almost the color of a hazelnut wolf.

The black wolf nipped at the brown ones tail playfully till the brown one took a quick turn causing the black one to lose it's footing, tumble over and stand back up. The wolf shook off the leaves and everything started to fade out. The sound of leaves ruffling stayed with her.

Xavier was carrying Haley through the woods with the sound of crunching leaves under his rather large feet. Haley started to wiggle in his arms as everything was black but she heard leaves. Feeling the cool gust of wind her eyes shot open. The twos eyes connected and she immediately started to squirm and push at the strange mans large chest in attempt to get away.

Xavier's grip only tightened as she thrashed about. She finally stopped as it had got her no advantage and she was tired.

"Bona Puella." Xavier's deep voice rumbled over her. (Good girl)

Haley was completely freaked out at this point. She could hardly see the man carrying her.

Who is he? How did he find me? What did he say? Why does he want me? Were unanswered questions running through Haley's head.

Within a few minutes a car rolled to a stop in front of them and the Xavier opened the back door. Haley was put in the back seat and buckled up before Xavier was sat in the front.

Still very tired Haley looked over to read the clock on the dash. It was two thirty eight in the morning. Haley didn't know what to do as she had never been kidnapped, she had no way to even communicate with them and the option of them knowing sign language was completely out of the question. So Haley made the best decision in her mind to get comfortable in her seat with her head leaned against the window and her legs curled up behind the seat belt with her body. Slowly she started to doze off.

~KARL DREXEL from ottomodels.com

AN: I'm graduating tomorrow!!! So excited! But for I have a straight face typing this. So tired from grad night #chronicallyill

Anyways happy reading my loves

Vote and comment

11

- -

C hapter 11

Haley had woken up in a soft warm bed as the thought of the two weird dreams she had. She opened her eyes to look around wanting to see what time it was when they landed on a muscular man in a big arm chair on the side of the bed her alarm clock would be. That's when Haley realized this isn't her room and she didn't know that man.

Haley sat up scooting away from the man with the covers halfway covering her petite pajama clad body.

"Amare, it's okay." Xavier's deep voice came out as he stood from his previous sitting position. (Love)

Haley vigorously shook her head trying to get away from the tall, dark, intimidating stranger who looked like he could break Haley's small frame with just a touch of his little finger. Xavier made his way towards the unnamed girl that he only knew as his mate as she continued shaking her head. Haley stood from the bed in attempt to create distance and back away from him. The cold air hit Haley's cream colored skin after she stepped from the blanket.

"Vos es ok infans." Xavier spoke softly lightly reaching his hand out to Haley. (You're Okay baby)

Haley continued to shake her head out of fear as she backed herself into a corner of the wall. Now shivering from the cold Haley curled into a small ball sitting on the floor with her eyes closed wishing everything that was happening and had happened away like it never happened or was a thought in anyone's mind.

Xavier noticed that his mate was shivering. He pulled the comforter from the bed and gently laid it on the small shaking figure on the floor in the corner.

This took Haley by surprise and she looked up to meet soft speckled brown eyes the color of a dark chocolate cake with a milk chocolate frosting. They were a beautiful mix of different shades of Haley's favorite color.

Brown.

Haley took this time to examine Xavier even though she could stare into his sparkling eyes all the time. She found him to be dressed in dark denim jeans and a long sleeve button up shirt that was rolled up showing his thick muscular forearms. Xavier bent down to Haley's level and sat in front of her. She thought she had seen this man before but didn't have a clue from where or who he was.

"What's your name?" He asked light taking in the dark messy hair that was once beautifully curled and the smudged makeup around Haley's eyes.

He thought she was breathtakingly beautiful even with these few flaws.

Haley didn't respond to this as she didn't speak. With a moment of silence more Xavier spoke again.

"How old are you?" He was louder and more demanding now that his first question went unanswered unsure if she didn't hear or just didn't answer.

His volume made Haley jump slightly. He huffed angrily as Haley now looked at the floor.

"Do you even speak?! Stercore!" He yelled now standing but still looking at Haley. (Shit)

Flinching Haley shook her head fiercely as it was the first question she could answer.

"You don't speak?" He asked much more calm as he finally caught on.

Haley clarified by shaking her head once again.

"Why?" He voiced once again louder than before "Did someone hurt you?!" His eyes now a deep dark brown as he got mad.

Haley one again shook her head.

"It's by choice?" He asked confused as she nodded.

There was a long pause filled with silence while Xavier was thinking. Haley was still cold and slightly shaking but conjured up enough courage to slowly stand. She took small step forward with the blanket still wrapped around her. Xavier intensely watched her as she took her final step up to him. She reached out with one hand slowly reaching for his shirt as the other held the blanket. She grabbed lightly onto his shirt and pulled it gently to her as she asked for clothes.

Xavier's big hand softly wrapped around the small hand Haley used to ask with. He pulled her into to his closet that was filled completely with different types of men's clothes. Haley looked around finding his jackets and hoodies. She pulled it off of the hanger dropping the blanket to the floor as she slipped into it. She then looked around for shorts or pants but found they would all be to big around her hips as well as for her legs. So she settled for socks she found in the drawer and pulled them on welcoming any kind of warmth.

Xavier stood in the doorway of the closet observing Haley's every move. She pulled the blanket up and turned to him.

"Do you need anything?" He asked softly as multiple emotions flashed through his eyes.

Haley motioned as if she was writing something down with her right hand causing Xavier to nod and turned. He walked out of the room down the hall as Haley followed him. They entered an office and he walked around the desk. He grabbed a piece of paper and a pen setting then next to him as he sat down in the rolling chair. He sat forward in the chair as he watched Haley write her first question standing next to him.

'Who are you?'

"I'm Xavier Daron. What's your name?"

'Haley. Why am I here?' A growl came from him before he spoke to a questioning Haley.

"You're mine. I'm keeping you safe here."

'Yours? Where are the Devin's? Are they okay?'

"Yes. They're fine at their home."

'Can I go home?'

"No! You are home!" He boomed as Haley flinched away.

He let out a sigh and spoke again.

"Are you hungry?"

Haley nodded as he started walking through the house. They ended up in the kitchen when Xavier got Haley a glass of water and she picked up a banana from the fruit bowl.

~AN: omg I'm getting so bad at this!!! I know it's Thursday forgive me. New chapter up only for more days of my summer left

Vote and comment

12

- -

A N: Xavier's beta Reid

Chapter 12

Haley got full halfway through the banana and set it down. Taking a sip of water Xavier studied her from across the counter.

"Oh she's awake!" The unknown man boomed excitedly as he entered the room which started Haley.

She looked over at the man who was not as big or as muscular as Xavier but he was still quite intimidating especially if he was not compared to Xavier. She had placed him as the driver of the car that they had took her in earlier this morning.

Reid stood tall at about six foot one. His face was sharp and well defined. He had average sized lips and a long nose that freckles ran across and onto his hollowed cheeks which pronounced his cheekbones greatly. He had dark eyebrows that hovered over his dark hazel eyes surrounded by long black eyelashes. He had dark brown hair that was disheveled as if he only ran his hands though it in the morning.

Xavier replied to his observation with a head nod and then both men left while talking, leaving Haley alone in the kitchen. The two men went to the office talking about things like the pack, any threats, or rouges.

Haley got up from the chair and started to wonder aimlessly around the house. She found different rooms around the house as she let her mind consume her with thoughts. Xavier came to mind. He was quite handsome and seemed to be nice as he tried to provide her some warmth and food. But what slightly scared Haley was his short temper that went off at almost anything that he didn't like and the fact that he kidnapped her.

She didn't like that he took her and just dropped her in this unfamiliar place that Haley had never seen or even heard of before.

Haley was pulled out of though as she opened a door just a few doors down from the bedroom she was previously sleeping in.

There was a giant shiny black piano that caught Haley's attention when she opened the door. She was immediately drawn to it and she pulled out the bench seat sitting down in the middle of it. She delicately removed the cover from the keys and lightly ran her fingers over the unworn and most likely untouched keys as she admired its prestige condition. Her slim fingers pressed a few keys individually while thinking of what her mom used to say about listening to each sound of the note as she first learned how to play the piano. A tear slipped down her cheek and landed on one of the keys as she thought of her deceased mother.

Haley pulled the cover back over the keys knowing she couldn't deal with those emotions on top of the ones she was already feeling with being in this unfamiliar place. She also didn't want to get in trouble for touching the piano now that she thought about it.

Haley walked out and wandered back to the room that she had woken up in. She laid down in the bed soon drifting off to sleep without realizing she was even tired.

*

It had been two days staying with Xavier and not seeing the Devin's. Haley had started to miss them and the bacon and potatoes that was a regular food in the house even if she hardly ate much of it. Haley turned over looking at the clock and it read one twenty four. The soft breathing next to Haley came from Xavier who would come in after Haley fell asleep and he would sleep next to her. It made her feel a little weird as he was still basically a stranger but he made her feel safe and warm just being around him at the same time so she dismissed the thoughts of completely pushing him away.

Haley got up as she was not able to fall back asleep from the weird dream she couldn't seem to remember now. She wandered out of the room letting her body do what it may till she found herself in the same guest room that she was in a few days ago. She started to touch the keys and it was like a dam broke.

She started to cry hysterically as she plays her mothers favorite song which also happened to be the last one she had learned, "secret lover". She remembered her mom telling her the story behind why it happened to be her favorite song.

Her mother Hadlee and father Jake were almost like secret lovers the way they had always liked each other and kept their relations out of sight because people didn't always approve for an unknown reason to Haley. Also a guy claimed to really like Hadlee but was mentally crazy and could possibly do anything crazy and hurt a loved one which Hadlee did not like the ideal of.

Haley sobbed as her fingers danced in the piano keys with a mind of their own. With the last note floating through the air she put her face in her warm hands. The arms of Xavier wrapped around Haley's waist making her flinch. Tingles and little lightning bolts shot through their bare skin as it brushed against each other.

"Denique te amare." Was whispered in Haley's ear as she was picked up from her seat and now sat in Xavier's lap curled against his chest. (Your fine love)

He rubbed her back soothingly as she continued to cry into his bare chest. Xavier picked his mate up carrying her with him as he walk to his office. Haley sniffles softly in his lap as he pulled a pen and paper in front of her so she could respond to his questions.

"What's wrong?" Xavier asked as his voice filled with concern and worry.

'I wanna go back home.' A tear dropped on Haley's note as she wrote.

~AN: here's just another one bc I apologize for not remembering yesterday.

13

C hapter 13

"What's wrong?" Xavier asked as his voice filled with concern and worry.

'I wanna go back home.' A tear dropped on Haley's note as she wrote.

Xavier visibly stiffened under Haley as he shook his head no.

'Please take me to the Devin's.' Haley looked to him with a tear streaming down her face.

She had only known him for just days but she could already tell that he was silently having an internal battle with himself over what to do. He reluctantly gave a soft nod telling her that they could go.

"When?" He asked with a deep voice not likening this idea as she was his.

His mate. His Luna. His girl. His weakness. His Joy. His pain. He owned her in his own odd but loving way.

'Now.'

With a sigh Xavier lifted Haley's petite frame, carrying her back into the bedroom. He quickly pulled on a shirt and jeans and then turned to Haley. He found a big jacket to go over his big shirt and her small night shorts she had on from three nights ago when he took her. Xavier also helped her into his large socks and he pulled her up while tucking her into his side for comfort and warmth.

Haley hiccuped softly walking down the halls with him. He opened a door leading into a large and spacious three car garage. Xavier opened Haley's door, buckling her into the seat and got into the driver side doing the same for himself.

Soft hiccups filled the silent car as Xavier sped to the house that Haley had only spent about a month in since moving from Washington. Xavier lifted Haley out of the car and she buried her head in his neck as he carried her and walked up to the porch. His large fist rapped on the door at a fast pace.

Steven only had on his Flannel pajama pants as he stood at the door with his wife in a blush night gown behind him. Haley moved her head and saw Bethany. She slowly slipped down from Xavier's hold walking in the house.

Xavier and Steven glare at each other as Tyson walked down the stairs following his fathers actions. As Haley reached Bethany her tears started to flow heavily again. Beth soothingly ran her hands through Haley's tangled wavy hair. The three men were talking but Haley completely blocked it out with her crying.

After a short while Haley's tears had dried up and she pulled back from Bethany. The talking had stopped as Haley looked over to Tyson who had an upset but saddened look on his face. He opened his arms and they hugged each other closely. A growl came from the door where Xavier stood with fist clenched and dark eyes boring into Tyson's.

"What happened?" Xavier asked with authority in his voice and Bethany, Tyson, and Haley walk into the kitchen.

Bethany pulled a pen and paper from the counter sliding it to Haley.

'I miss them.'

Bethany nodded kissing Haley's head as Tyson stood behind her rubbing her back.

"Hot cocoa baby?" Bethany asked Haley as she slightly nodded.

Everyone was now in the kitchen and Xavier had read the note that his mate had just wrote.

"Who?" Xavier's voice flowed through the room.

As no one answered Xavier walked over to Haley who was sitting at the kitchen table. He picked her up off the seat and sat down with her in his lap.

"Who do you miss deliciae?" He asked softly. (Darling)

Both Tyson and Steven growled at them as their wolf didn't like their little girl being touched by a man let alone sitting in his lap. Haley bent forward to start writing but stopped when Xavier boomed out to the two men.

"I can touch my mate if I want!"

Haley looked back confused and raised a questioning eyebrow at him and then the family. No one made eye contact with her and Xavier had stiffened while shaking his head. She had nodded understanding that it might be a personal thing and people need time. Bethany handed the cocoa to Haley and she started to sip the warm drink.

"Are you okay?" Bethany asked Haley again talking about everything over all not just her family or just Xavier.

Haley shrugged halfheartedly and lightly nodded as Tyson and Xavier continued to glare at each other until interrupted by a small growl coming from Steven. He then stepped forward from his position next to his son.

"Do you want to stay the night?" He asked and Xavier moved his sight over to growl at Steven.

'I just miss you guys and them.' Haley wrote.

Everyone looked at the note.

"You can always stay when you want." Steven spoke up again to comfort of the closet thing to his daughter.

"No!" Xavier yelled and stood pulling Haley to him closely.

All men were glaring at each other as Bethany looked to Haley. She rubbed her arm reassuringly telling her it was okay.

"Alpha Daron? Will you let her come see us when she wants? If she wants to stay you can too. She's been through some stuff and she need something familiar sometimes." Bethany spoke softly with a sad smile.

"What happened?!" His voice boomed behind Haley.

She shook her head not ready to tell a man who took her from her home and and family to stay with him.

"She will explain to you when she's ready. Give her time." Haley nodded and finished the cocoa.

She hugged the people she considered family earning a growl, dark eyes, and shaking clench fists from Xavier. She turned to him and yawned while nodding for him to follow her as she made her way up the stairs into the old bedroom.

Haley didn't understand why Bethany called Xavier Alpha or why the three men continuously growled at each other like animals. But that was the least of her thoughts as she laid down in the double bed tired of crying and ready to sleep. The bed dipped and tingles ran the skin of her back as Xavier's hand rubbed soothing circles.

"We'll go home tomorrow amare." Xavier spoke softly as Haley fell asleep. (Love)

14

C hapter 14

Haley woke up in the morning and started to stretch out her limbs when she hit something. She heard a groan and realized it wasn't a wall but looked to see that she had hit a sleeping Xavier. Haley quietly crawled out of bed and got clothes from her closet. She went to the bathroom to take a shower and change and then she went down stairs into the kitchen. Natalie and Bethany were in the kitchen and greeted her. Natalie sent a big white smile to Haley who returned it with a nod.

"Good morning honey. Are you okay?" Bethany asked as she set a plate of has browns in front of Haley and eggs in front of Natalie.

Haley ate about half the plate which really surprised her and Bethany. Tyson came into the kitchen rubbing Haley's head and kissing her forehead. Haley hugged him showing that she missed him. They pulled apart and he walked over to Natalie and kissed her. Haley liked how happy the two seemed just in each other's presence. Tyson looked behind Haley as he sat down and shook his head.

"We have to go home. Let's get you some of your clothes." Xavier spoke and caused Bethany to frown.

Grabbing the paper that was left of the table from last night Haley started to write.

'What about school?'

"Oh honey you don't need to go. I will take care of everything." Bethany nodded to Xavier who nodded back.

Haley went to her room and started to pick out a few clothes. She didn't own a lot and some stuff didn't fit anymore so it was quite easy for her to pick out her favorite things. She walked down stairs with a bag in hand holding half of her wardrobe.

Everyone was waiting down stairs for Haley. She hugged them all including Natalie. Steven whispered that she could come over any time in his hug. Then Xavier and Haley got into the car leaving back to Xavier's pack.

Nothing happened for the next few days. Xavier would come to bed late and leave early before Haley woke up. When Haley did see him during the day he would always pull her to him or into his lap. Haley thought it was weird at first but now she enjoys his touch and feeling of safety from just being around him.

This morning Xavier had already left to his office when he got a report of rogues crossing into his territory. They caught them all and brought them to a place similar to a prison where Xavier questioned each one of them. He had beat the men but kept them alive as they didn't answer anything and might possibly have answers later on.

While Xavier was handling the rouges a warlock slipped past completely unseen and he was heading straight for Xavier's house. Like the rouges he was on a mission. A mission to get a message to Haley.

Haley was still sound asleep in the room but that was perfect for the warlock as he preferred to be unseen and he could now do whatever he wanted because she was asleep.

He was now in the room looking at the wild hair of a sleeping Haley. The warlock was to just tell Haley about the danger she would be facing and to watch out if she wanted to stay alive, but that would be to simple. He wanted to cause her some type of physical pain for making him go through the loss of his son all cause by Haley's father. Real father.

Haley woke up so see a note on the bedside table. She looked at it and frowned.

It read. 'You have caused this chaos and you will soon wish you were never conceived. Watch your back or fall into my trap.'

No one has signed it and it made no scenes to Haley so she ignored it thinking it could possibly be a joke and was definitely not for her, as she sat up. An excruciating pain shot up her side causing her to fall back with a whimper. She removed the sheets to see what happened to find the sheets stained a crimson red.

Xavier had just beat several rogues. As he walked back to his home because he got a scenes of something wrong. He didn't know what or why but he hurried back looking for his mate who was dizzy and starting to go unconscious from loss of blood. He ran up to his room finding a shallow breathed Haley bleeding out in their bed.

He mind linked his beta and the pack doctor to come to his house. His beta Reid arrived almost immediately and the doctor was soon behind him. He ran in getting straight to work by removing her shirt. Xavier was not a fan of this action but controlled himself knowing the doctor was here to help his mate.

The wound was cleaned and green ooze started to seep out of it. The doctor stopped his work and just stared. He had seen this before and out of the only three times he saw this in his life one out of the three survived. They had only made it six months after.

Pack doctor Stewart knew he had about an hour or so before she goes into shock and dies on the spot but he had nothing to cure her here.

"Pick her up we're going to the infirmary now. We need to hurry." He spoke quickly but calm.

Xavier picked her up with the bedsheets covering her body. They rushed to the infirmary where she was laid down on a bed.

Doctor Stewart asked both men to leave as the Alpha would possibly rip him apart for extracting the venomous ooze and burning his mate to kill whatever was left in her and sealing everything together.

Reid and Xavier sat outside of the room waiting for anything. Laura, Reid's mate came walking into the infirmary looking for her mate and Alpha because she started to worry when eight hours had passed without any sign form ether of them.

She slowly walked in and sat on the opposite side of her mate with her hand on Xavier's shoulder. She had no clue what was running through his head and she could never imagine being in his position but she thought of him as an older brother that she had to show love and support too.

"It will be okay, she's strong. She has to be if she's mated to you. Take your mind off of it. Go home. Get cleaned up and eat something. I know your starving. Reid will go with you. I'll stay here with her and mind link you if anything happens." She spoke quietly in her motherly and convincing voice.

"I can't leave her." Xavier's deep voice was horse and raspy.

"Yes. You still need to take care of yourself because there is a pack that needs you. There's nothing you can do for her right now. I'll be here." She finally convinced him as he nodded his head lightly still reluctant to leave but knowing his pack needed him.

Xavier huffed standing up with Reid following him. Reid lightly kissed Laura and walked to the pack house. About ten to fifteen minutes later Doctor Stewart walked out looking tired and held a sad, weak smile.

"She's gotta be okay doc." Laura said knowing their ruthless Alpha would become dead inside if anything happened to his mate.

~AN: will Haley be okay?!?!?! Omg!!!

Laura in media

15

- -

Chapter 15

Doctor Stewart walked out looking tired and held a sad, weak smile.

"She's gotta be okay doc." Laura said knowing their ruthless Alpha would become dead inside if anything happened to his mate.

"She's asleep right now. She should wake up anytime. If she sits up make sure it's slowly." He nodded to Laura knowing who she is as beta female.

She nodded thanking him and sat in the room with Haley. Laura was not going to tell Xavier till Haley at least woke up. She knew he needed some type of rest and he could still do nothing at this point.

Xavier had found the note in his room when they got home. He called Reid in to see if he knew anything about this. Which they both didn't. They set it on the back burner while they knew Haley healing was more important.

Two hours later Haley started to move and mumble incoherently. She made a grunting sound as a pain shot up her side as she was now waking up.

With a few more grumbles Laura decided to stand up incase Haley made the rash decision to sit up.

Which she did. Immediately.

"Slowly. Slowly sit up. It's okay." Laura cooed helping Haley and moving the pillows around.

Haley only gave Laura a questioning look as she had never seen this woman and didn't know where she was.

"Let me get you some paper and I'll explain everything, okay?" Laura smiled again making Haley feel oddly comfortable and somewhat safe with the stranger.

Laura handed the napkin and pen to Haley as it was all that she had found but knowing it would be their only communication from talking with Reid. Haley immediately went to writing, carefully of her sore side.

'Who are you?'

"I'm Laura. Reid's girlfriend. I'm sure you've seen him around with Xavier before."

'What am I doing here? Why does my side hurt?'

"Well there was a doctor fixing you up not to long ago. I think your side was cut so Xavier brought you here."

Haley nodded and they sat in silence for a little.

'Where's Xavier?' Haley wrote.

"I made him go home, shower, and rest. Do you want me to call him for you?" Laura asked politely.

Haley nodded in response and Laura walked out to mind link Xavier so Haley wouldn't question if she called him.

"Alpha Xavier. She's awake now." Xavier immediately replied with an okay.

As Xavier and Reid were walking in the doors they previously walked out of hours ago when Doctor Stewart caught Xavier. Xavier told Reid to go and he'd catch up.

"Yes Doctor?"

"Alpha, anytime I have seen what happened to a patient they die. Two have died instantly and one died six months later. She seems to be good and better than anyone I've ever seen. Her body seemed to reject the venom that was in her side but I can't say none got in. She should be healthy but I cannot promise you that." Stewart spoke timidly to his Alpha.

"Thank you." Xavier's voice was deeper than usual as he took in that his mate could die soon.

He hurried to the room wanting to see her. When he walked in Haley was laying down with her eyes closed as Reid and Laura spoke lightly.

Haley heard the door open and looked to see who it was. Xavier walked over to where she was laying. He picked up her hand and gave it a gentle squeeze.

Haley took in the warmth that spread through her body with his touch. She closed her eyes contently as goosebumps flooded her skin from his electric current that flow through their hands.

Xavier leaned down to kiss her head. As he was pulling back he bent down to her ear and whispered.

"How are you doing deliciae?" His warm breath fanned her ear and neck causing a shiver to run down her spine. (Darling)

She nodded her head softly saying that she was okay. Even though her side was killing her.

The rest of the day Xavier stayed by Haley's side. Laura and Reid left about thirty minutes or so after Xavier had walked in. Haley stayed the night in the room with Xavier sleeping in the chair next her her. Haley had disapproved and made that clear as she wrote that he should go home. The next day Haley was released from the infirmary and went back to the house.

*

A few days later Haley hadn't really done anything beside sleep, stay in the room, or sit on Xavier's lap as he works. Xavier work on papers for the pack all day as he was catching up with the two days he missed.

Right now Haley was looking through the window longing for fresh air. She got dressed and went to find Xavier. He was in his office as usual when Haley found him with Reid facing him.

"Gunners an old man who can't do anything to my pack." Was the stiff reply of Xavier as she walked around the desk and grabbed a scratch piece of paper.

Xavier lightly pulled her down into his lap mindful of her still achy side. The conversation between Reid and Xavier had ceased and they now payed attention to the quick writing of Haley.

'Can we go outside?'

There was a long pause.

"Only around the house." Xavier nodded softly as he locked into Haley's pleading eyes.

She nodded and they all three stood. They walked down the halls to the front door with Xavier leading the way and Reid in the back. They walked outside a light breeze passed by them as the sun was shining down.

Xavier turned left once outside and walked Haley to a garden. The men stopped as Haley walked around taking in the yellow of leaves with the plush green grass around all the plants. Haley admired the vines crawling up the trellis with colors of forest green, shades of orange, and dull browns.

"I have to go there's rouges on the territory." Xavier said to Reid as it came to the ears of Haley but didn't process.

Reid quickly walked over to Haley drawing her attention to him. She saw Xavier storming off in another direction.

"We have to go. Xavier will be back, we will wait in his office." Reid said lightly taking the wrist of Haley to quickly pull her into safety.

~

AN: rouges? Why would I do that!!

First day of class was a success. On to day two.

16

C hapter 16

"We have to go. Xavier will be back, we will wait in his office." Reid said lightly taking the wrist of Haley to quickly pull her into the safety of the home instead of outside.

About forty five minutes had passed with Reid working on pack papers at Xavier's desk and in his chair. Haley was laying on the couch letting her mind flow and now process what Xavier said.

Something with rouges but Haley was pretty sure that the word rogue meant it was a reddish color. Also territory, the way he said it, like he had and owned a big place or piece of land around and was in charge of it. Then she was thinking about multiple things that he had said in the past but one stuck out that she still didn't have the answer to. Mates.

Not very long later Xavier walked in looking tired and somewhat dirty. Reid got out of the chair with a nod, walking around the desk for his Alpha to sit down.

Xavier walked over to Haley before he went to sit down and grabbed her hand lightly pulling her with him as she followed. He sat down in the big office chair and pulled her into his lap. Once settled he put his nose in her neck and hair taking a big whiff in. Immediately he calmed down and relaxed into the chair. The two men continued on paper work for a while longer then Reid left for the night saying he had to get to Laura.

Xavier finished a few more papers then leaned back into the chair with his eyes closed. His hand was on Haley's hip and thigh holding her to him. With his hand underneath the hem of her shirt he rubbed light circles with his thumb over her hipbone sending chills to shoot all over her body and was replaced with warmth as he continued.

Haley studied him for a while, while he had his eyes closed. She was taking in all his features from the length of his eyelashes, to the bump on the bridge of his nose. Haley though that he had truly handsome features and some slightly added to his intimidating demeanor.

His eyes slowly fluttered open to catch Haley staring. He grabbed a piece of clean paper and put it in front of her.

"What were you thinking about?" He asked softly and a small smile crossed his lips.

'What are mates?' Haley spelled out quickly sliding the paper into his view.

"Mate is like a soulmate, someone your supposed to be with and spend the rest of your life with because their your other half." He spoke softly but knowledgeable.

Haley though for a second before she continued to write as more questions filled her brain.

'I'm your mate?'

"Yes."

'That's why I stay with you?'

"Yes."

Haley nodded understanding the answers to the questions she had asked. She leaned back into Xavier's chest getting comfortable in his radiating warmth. She closed her eyes and let her mind roam till she slipped off to sleep.

*

Haley woke up with a startle. A loud crash is what caused her to wake up. Another crash soon followed. Haley sat up on the bed now realizing that Xavier had took her to their room to sleep. Another crash came echoing through the house that scared Haley but it made her curious as Xavier was not in the room with her like usual. She looked to the time as she stood up seeing that it was twelve fifty seven.

Walking out of the room she followed the continuous sound of crashing. A loud growl ripped through the air as she walked up to the wood door that was pushed to. Cautiously she walked down the halls toward Xavier's office. Only heavy breathing sounded through the room so Haley decided it should be okay to walk in with no crashing sounds coming.

Pushing the door a little more she poked her head in to see a giant mess with papers everywhere and things knocked over. Her eyes then found Xavier who was facing away from her as his breathes come out hard and unsteady. His torso was bare and his fist were tightly balled at his sides.

Haley slowly started to approach the heavy breathing man, attentive to broken things on the floor. She rest her small hand on Xavier's bare tense back. He stiffened and flinched as she walked around him to stand face to face.

His eyes were pitch black with light hints of gold around as he cast his eyes down to the floor. Haley noticed and she knew that this wasn't the Xavier she grew to like and know. This was a man completely different and she wanted the one she started to have feeling for back.

Gradually Haley wrapped her arms around Xavier's waist under his arms. She laid her head in his chest trying to ignore the tingles and warmth shooting through her. Xavier's erratic heart beat started to slow down into a steady rhythm under Haley's ear.

Haley looked up to see that this eyes were closed as he took steady breathes in and out. She placed a light smooth kiss onto the spot where his heart was now rhythmically beating at a stable pace.

Xavier lifted his arms from hanging at the sides of his body to wrap around the frail body of Haley. He slowly picks her up as she clung to him laying her head down in the crook of his neck. She breathed in his strong scent as he walks out still carrying Haley. She was gently placed down onto the bed and rolls to her side. The opposite side of the bed dipped and a heavy arm wraps around her waist pulling her into the warm muscular chest of Xavier.

A slight smile grows on Haley's lips as she knew she had made some sort of progress with Xavier as he got the hint of her wanting him in bed. He also came to bed with her without either one saying anything.

C hapter 17

When Haley woke up, snoring was heard right above her ear as she had ended up with her head resting on Xavier's hard tan chest. She turned slightly and Xavier instinctively wrapped his arms tighter around Haley's waist as he was still asleep. She would have felt guilty to wake him up so she turned laying her head over his steady beating heart. She placed a soft kiss over the sound that was like a lullaby soothing her. Xavier woke up finally releasing his grip from her waist.

"Good morning love." Xavier deep sleep filled voice flowed through the room.

Haley nodded kissing his cheek as her way of saying it back. He went into the bathroom taking a shower while Haley got dressed. They switched with Xavier getting Dressed and Haley in the bathroom.

Haley walked out as Xavier was pulling his shirt over his head. He walked over to her and interlocked their fingers. Holding hands Xavier lead them down into the kitchen.

Haley walked around the kitchen with Xavier as they both got breakfast. Haley got a small bowl of cereal as Xavier made himself eggs.

He had finished making his breakfast and turned to the island. Haley was sitting on a bar stool on the opposite side of where Xavier stood to eat. The house was silent besides the two eating.

Haley pulled a note pad that was made for grocery lists down from the fridge and took the magnetic pen that was beside it. She sat back down across from Xavier and pushed her bowl aside to start writing.

'What happened last night?' Haley flipped the note around and pushed it to Xavier.

"A friend died." He spoke in a deep voice looking down with his eyes shut.

Haley reached her hand out to place it on the giant, tense one of Xavier. She rubbed small relaxing circles on the back of Xavier's tan skin. His shoulders dropped down at the touch of his mate making him feel all okay, like the weight of his pack and what's been going on has been lifted off his shoulders.

Xavier went up to his office once he finished eating and started more work. Haley finished her cereal and washed the dishes. She found herself randomly walking into Xavier office. She lays down on the couch in the corner with her head on the arm rest.

Haley woke up in the same position as Reid and Laura walked in. No one realized she was awake as they talked. She stayed still laying on the couch just listening to their conversation.

Reid has said something about someone named Alpha Gunner, a name Haley had heard briefly before, and Laura explain how he was never up to good.

"I mean it's weird how Alpha Gunner asked for land and then when you told him no, rouges started to attack. And what also seems weird to me is how Haley got here and Gunner started contacting you more which seemed to coincide with the rouge attacks as they always happened to be right after you deny his offer. I mean didn't he even ask who your mate was at one point?" Laura introduced on the stagnant conversation between Xavier and her mate.

"Alpha Gunner wants control over you to get Haley. That's where the note came from." Reid said as if he had just found out the deepest secret without anyone telling him.

"NO ONE WILL TAKE MY MATE. Qui tries me interficere dimisi ut tangeres eam." Xavier's tone went from yelling to deadly. (I will kill whoever tries to touch her)

Haley didn't like when Xavier was mad, sad, or upset. She's always felt a pull towards him when he was feeling something like that.

Haley sat up from the laying position she was in. She rubbed the sleep out of her eyes as she walked over to Xavier. His intense gases was fixed on her as her small frame approached him.

As Haley passed Laura and Reid, all eyes were on her in this silent moment. Xavier had rolled back in his chair so Haley could fit in his lap between the desk. Once she was standing in front of Xavier he thought she would turn to sit on his lap like usual so it surprised him when she kneeled onto the chair straddling his legs.

With her butt resting mid thigh on Xavier she wrapped her arms around his neck as she cradled her head there too. She left a small kiss right in the crease where Xavier's neck met his shoulder.

A shiver of pleasure shot down his spine as his wolf purred in joy and ecstasy. Haley did it one more time enjoying his reaction and then she pulled back.

"I'm sorry for waking you up." Xavier soft words came which shocked his Beta and his Beta's mate as the two had never seen this much of the soft loving side of Xavier that they were seeing now.

Haley shook her head telling him that he was not the cause of her waking up. She leaned down to give Xavier a kiss on the cheek but caught the side of his lips. She pulled back with wide eyes and blushed profusely. Immediately she snapped her head down embarrassed at her actions.

A deep chuckle rumbled through Xavier's chest as the two on the opposite side of his desk snickered. He had mind linked the two that they should go home for the day. They silently left the office without Haley knowing.

Xavier slid his index finger under the chin of Haley to bring her head up. As she looked up she tried to yield her eyes to another direction scared and nervous of making contact with him.

"Look at me... It's okay. I am yours and only yours to do with as you'd like. I would enjoy a kiss on the lips whenever you are ready my sweet mate." Xavier spoke reassuringly as Haley's eyes lead back to his own.

Xavier leaned in kissing the forehead of Haley after brushing a few curly wild strands out of the way. He rested his forehead on hers and took in her scent.

Xavier no doubt had strong feelings for Haley at this point in time but he didn't know if it was love or not. He knew it was something stronger than lust or liking just by looking at her when he wakes up. Her wild black hair stuck up in some places and her big eyes held sleep but that was part of her flaw full beauty. She never dressed up or tried to impress anyone at all which he was more than okay with. Xavier enjoyed how she would feel comfortable enough to not only place herself in his lap or arms but to pull him close and kiss him softly. He knew she was slowly letting him in and feeling the pull wether she knew it or not.

*

The next four days were very uneventful. Nothing happened in the pack, nothing happened in the house, and nothing happened around the territory.

Xavier and Haley were laying in bed with light snoring coming from Xavier for hours. That was not what was keeping Haley up.

What kept Haley up was her mind wandering and she couldn't do anything about it. She wondered who would have done that to her side, who would have killed her parent, what if she was awake when that happened to her side? Would she be dead now? What if it's the same person who killed her parents?

All these thoughts have kept her up for hours no matter how hard she tired to fall asleep. Tired of the warm breath fanning against the back of her head she decided to get up and go to the piano room. This was something she did a lot when her parents first died. It seemed to clear her mind for long enough to eventually get her to sleep or cry and fall asleep from exhaustion.

Sitting down on the black bench she let her fingers start touching the keys after she removed the cover. Before long Haley was humming a very familiar melody. It was one her mother would play for her every time she couldn't get to sleep at night as a little girl.

A rough hand pulled Haley from her thought free mind as it wrapped around her mouth startling her. She immediately started to thrash knowing it was not Xavier from no warmth and it didn't have Reid's distinct smell.

"Shhh. I'm not going to hurt you beautiful, but I can't say the same about your father. He's very upset with you mother and because she is not here the blame falls on you. This whole thing is about you." The scratchy voice spoke as nails dug into Haley's arm as the man tried to stop her movements.

Haley continued to thrash about and when the grip tightened over her mouth and nose cutting off oxygen and cutting her cheek she pounded on the piano as she tried to break free. Salty tears rolled quickly down her cheeks as fear consumed her that she may not make it out of this.

A growl ripped through the dark room, the same growl that Haley heard when Xavier's friend died but this one was much more threatening. The tight grip of the man was torn off of Haley. She turned to see Xavier on top of the older creepy looking man throwing punch after punch.

Haley instantly scrunched up in a tinny ball in the corner of the room till everything became silent. There was no growls or snarls. There was no punching or bone cracking. There wasn't even heavy breathing. There was a small whimper that left Haley's lips then a heavy breath released and loud footsteps. The steps stopped right in front of her.

A hand reached out and touched Haley's arm causing her to flinch into the corner more.

"It's okay infantem puella." Xavier's voice was soft as tingles ran through Haley's arm. (Baby girl)

Xavier bent down to pick her up, she curled into his warm chest crying harder as she now felt comforted and safe in the arms of Xavier. He placed delicate kissed on the wet cheek of Haley as he walked them into the bathroom after mind linking Reid to take care of the body.

Haley was set on the sink counter and Xavier started the bath. He washed his bloody hands in the sink as Haley watched the bubbles rise in the tub with tears still in her eyes. Xavier stood right in front of Haley lightly tugging and lifting the hem of her shirt. She had nothing on underneath but she was still in to much shock to care or even realize. Xavier continued by pulling down her shorts leaving her completely bare. He picked Haley up setting her in the water. Not long later the water sloshed in the tub and was turned off by Xavier who just got in behind Haley.

Even with Xavier's mate naked in front of him he never had a corrupt thought of her in this vulnerable state she was in.

He pulled her back into his chest and little electrons ran through her body with Xavier's warm touch. Haley was covered with bubbles just past her small chest.

"Pulchra." Was whispered into the hair of Haley. (Beautiful)

Haley breathed in Xavier's intoxicating but soothing scent as it surrounded her for she was on Xavier's lap which he always seemed to like.

18

C hapter 18

   The next morning Xavier had woken up early to find out any information about that man before his mate woke up and faced the reality of it. He was also going to have to question her and he wanted to find out as much as possible to not only take care of what went on but to see if Haley is lying or telling the truth. Xavier needs to be able to trust his mate and the pack their Luna but there was never a situation like this for a test till now.

Haley woke up with the end of her hair damp. She put her hair in a bun getting ready and pulled out one of Xavier's shirts as his scent made her feel safe and at peace. She remembered everything vividly from last night till Xavier took her to the bathroom. After that it was foggy and she could only assume that Xavier dried her off, clothed her, and put her to bed, where she woke up, after that.

Once Haley was dressed she wondered to find Xavier. She didn't want any breakfast this morning. The event from last night seemed to shrink the size of her appetite to virtually nothing. Being here with Xavier eating every meal after Tyson had got her to eat more seemed to be improving her eating habits and health.

Haley opened the office door as that seemed to be the place to usually find Xavier or Reid if Xavier was out. Haley had peeked her head in to see Xavier already staring at her from across the room behind his desk as if he already knew she was going to be there, which he did with his werewolf's great sense of smell. He waved Haley in and told her to come sit down patting his lap.

Haley walked in and already found a notebook full of lined paper open to the first blank page and a blank ink pen sitting on top of it, all in front of Xavier on his desk. Haley sat diagonal on his lap as it seemed he was going to need her to respond but she wanted to be able to see him as he speaks.

"I'm gonna ask you some questions about last night just to see what you know. Okay?" Haley nodded looking at Xavier.

"Who was that guy?" He asked as his eyes flickered to a dark almost black color and gold to back to normal as his wolf was angry about the whole situation but he had to keep him at bay.

'I don't know who he was.'

"What did he say to you?" He asked again.

'My "father" is mad at my mom and because she is dead I will pay and my "father" won't be so gentle.'

"Why did you do that?" Xavier pointed to the quotes that Haley put around the word father.

'My mom and dad were killed nine months ago.' Haley looked down at her hands in her lap as she felt her mood drop think or even talking about her parents.

Xavier stiffened and his breath got heavier at the sensitive subject as he could feel the pain Haley felt going through it.

"Would you like to see the Devin's?" Xavier changed the subject which made Haley feel a little better.

She quickly nodded her head yes as they stood up. Xavier grabbed her hand as she followed him quickly through the house. Xavier pulled Haley to the garage and opened the car door for her. Once he got in he took off going well over the speed limit but Haley was oblivious. Not very long after, they arrived.

Xavier knocked viciously on the door while holding Haley's hand in his other. Natalie opened to door and smiled widely. The smiley woman went to pull Haley into a hug when Xavier pulled Haley behind him.

"We need to speak with Steven." Xavier bombed making the smile on Natalie's face drop a little.

"Yeah come on in." She brought the two in closing the door behind them and continued, "STEVEN HALEY IS HERE!"

Steven and Tyson came down the stairs together with happy grins on their face till they say Xavier. Both the men on the stairs nodded and turned to walk back up with Xavier trailing behind them now.

"Hey love, how are you?" Natalie asked pulling Haley into her arms and walking into the living room.

Haley only nodded in reply when they sat on the couch with Bethany on her right and Natalie on her left. No one said anything as they watched the show playing.

In Tyson's office the three men sat on couches all facing each other. Tyson was in a big arm chair, Xavier was on a love seat across from Tyson and

Steven was sitting on an ottoman leaning forward with his elbows on his knees.

"Haley was attacked last night in the house. The man was not a wolf, and had no scent anywhere. When I asked her about it this morning she said that her father was coming after her because her mother is dead. Haley explained to me how here mother and father were killed. I need help finding who is behind this all." Their was pain in Xavier's voice as he wanted his mate safe and always happy.

A heavy sigh came from Steven as he nodded to his son telling him to explain everything. With a deep breath Tyson started to speak about the people who raised his beloved sister.

"Hadlee, Haley's mother and Jake, Haley's father moved to the house in the outskirts of the city right next to us when Haley was about six months old. Then Hadlee had Haley who looked very similar but the features they did not share were the ones Jake and Haley shared ether. The two never had any resemblance but Jake raised her as his daughter. We know that Hadlee and Jake were not mates and only got married when Haley was young. It is quite possible that Jake is not her biological father, but we don't know that for sure. Though they were not mates they loved each other unconditionally without a problem or fight and showed the same love to Haley but never told her about werewolf's or anything of the sorts as she was always weaker and never changed. Haley does have grandparents in the Moonstone pack where both Hadlee and Jake were from. They may have more knowledge then us." Tyson informed Xavier only in the event to keep Haley safe.

"Do you happen to know the names of her grandparents? I would like to speak to them." Xavier spoke after a short silence.

"His name was Steve and I believe he was the Delta and his mate was Flora." Steven spoke up remembering the dinner they all had together.

"Thank you for the information. I will put it to use immediately and see what I can find." Xavier nodded shaking hands with two men that he wouldn't have a single positive thought of until his mate came from their family.

Xavier left down the stairs to find Haley laying on the couch with her head in Bethany's lap as she plaid with her hair. It reminded Xavier of watching a small child resting in her mother's comfort.

"Haley? Are you ready?" Xavier interrupted the silence.

Haley sat up hugging Bethany as she kissed the top of her head. The two girls hugged before Haley stood. Walking past Xavier she hugged Steven who carried out the same actions as Bethany. Lastly Haley and Tyson stood in front of one another.

'How are you doing? How is he?' Tyson signed making a string tug at the corner of Haley's lips.

'I'm okay. He's really nice. He likes to be close all the time. It's like he needs me with him.'

'He does need you with him. Your his second half. You calm and control him.' Haley nodded only partly understanding but taking Tyson's approval as she had started to grow feelings towards Xavier.

'I love you brother.'

'I love you too.' Tyson pulled Haley into a hug after his reply. She still found comfort in the once very familiar embrace but still found Xavier's more illecebrous.

19

C hapter 19

Haley and Xavier got into the car after the brief conversation that was not spoken in words between Tyson and Haley. Xavier sped home quickly as Haley observe the scenery around them. She was oblivious to how Xavier seemed so frustrated, or upset this time but it was clearly indicated by his death grip on the steering wheel. Xavier was going to have to leave Haley for a full day if not more. This enraged Xavier because it left the uncertainty of Haley being safe and protected while he was gone. But the circumstances had lead him to believe that leaving Haley with the Devin's was the best option for both of them.

They quickly arrived home with Xavier pulling the car back into the garage like he had left it. When the two exited the car Xavier was quick to walk around and take Haley's smaller hand in his. He opened the door into the house for them and led the way into the kitchen where a pack cook had made soup for them to eat for dinner.

Xavier pulled Haley into a seat and sat across from her as he set a bowl down in front of her. Haley's stomach turned within its self as the soup was set down. It wasn't that the soup was foul smelling or unappealing at all. Haley just didn't feel right with the situation at hand, without her knowing what it was, and made the very slim apatite she had diminish to nothing.

After a few bites that Xavier had took he decided to speak up.

"I have a lot of work that I need to do. You can go to bed." Xavier's words seemed to pierce Haley has he talked as if had never and would never care for her.

She only gave a slight nod partly upset with him. She had thought over how the work may be tedious and stress him out or perhaps he may have been tired and not realized the tone he held while speaking with Haley. She had made up a few other scenarios where Xavier cared for her still but had a issue at hand to deal with and caused the sharp tone of voice from him.

Haley stood from her seat without even touching the spoon or the bowl of soup. She turned and walked to the room that both of them shared. She took a relaxing shower and headed to bed as Xavier started his laborious work of contacting the Moonstone pack.

*

Haley had not eaten for a full day as her stomach clinched and rolled with her emotions over Xavier and a selcouth feeling that had washed upon her without even a small amount of real reasoning for it. Haley sighed as her body felt fatigued and corpulent. Deciding it would most likely be best to just go to bed early again that's what she did. There was no reason for her to stay up as she had no use around the house and Xavier clearly didn't need or want her in his presence as he had went to bed late after Haley and awoke long before she had got up for his spot was empty, cold, and straightened out.

As Haley fell into a light sleep Xavier let out a frustrated growl as he was tired of working through the extensive and prolonged process of getting access to the land and a time to be there. His wolf was not only upset at the mentally strenuous work but that his mate was not with him nor had he seen her for more then the brief moments she was asleep in bed before he convinced himself to leave the tingles of their touch to help ensure Haley's safety.

Xavier worked for about three more hours till he couldn't stand being in the same house as his mate without being able to see or touch her. His wolf was anxious to see her now that they had spent everyday of the past week together but haven't seen her for just over twenty four hours. To tired to even read another word as his brain seemed to pulsate in his skull he thought best of it if he just turn in for the night and start early in the morning again. His heavy steps thudded down the hall as he made his way into his room.

Haley had heard a door close subconsciously and the thundering footsteps of Xavier as he walked around their room. She rolled from her back to onto her side as Xavier watched her while he got undressed. Xavier pulled the covers of the bed back sliding in between the sheets, he laid on his side as his arm draped over the thin waist of Haley that was clad in a hooded sweatshirt that was over two sizes to big as it was Xavier's.

A pleasurable moan left the thin pale pink lips of Haley as Xavier's large rough hand found the exposed skin of the small of her lower lumbar region. The electric current ran through both of the bodies causing warmth to spread. This made Xavier's wolf content even with the amount of time they were not together. That did not mean that Xavier felt the same.

He was selfish and jealous. Selfish as in he would need more then just the touch and spreading warmth to keep him content and please him. He didn't know what she was doing today but he didn't care now that he had her in such close proximity. The jealous Alpha envied the air that surrounded her as it got to touch, hold, and caress her but he did not get that opportunity.

Xavier kissed the corner of Haley's lips as he restrained himself from smothering her with affection and stealing Haley's first kiss without her knowledge, approval or consent.

Xavier had then fallen asleep with Haley as his last thought.

*

Xavier had woken up early as he told himself too. He battled between staying in bed with the woman he was possibly falling for if he went to such great lengths just for some answers, waking up the elysian who slept beside him, and just leaving to get work done.

He had chose the later of the two causing alexithymia to flood through her as she woke up. She did not even change out of the simple pair of underwear and the oversized jacket when she a woke finding it definitely unnecessary to get dressed when she would not see Xavier. That also gave her no need to impress him, like she could with her cheap wardrobe any-ways.

Walking down the hall Xavier caught a whiff of the multiple citrus smells that radiated off of his most needed person assuring him the she was awake. He stopped his work to listen.

Hearing movement and what he believed was the refrigerator door close a smile slithered across his face like a lion finding its meal.

Feather like footsteps littered the floor. Xavier knew he could not take another day alone. So he called for Haley. The only response he got was footsteps. The door handle jiggled and Haley side stepped into the brown hues of the office.

"Come here." His voice was soft as he waved her over.

Haley stood next to Xavier with her hand folded in front of her. He pulled her down to his lap with a light 'umph' as he no longer envied the air for he was wrapped securely around her as if a butterfly was cocooned. He now sighed with content as he took a big breath in on Haley's neck. He let his warm breath fan her as frisson ran down her spine.

~~~~~~~~~~~~~~~~~~~~~~~~~~~~~Word you may not know in this chapter.

Selcouth- when everything feels strange

Corpulent- heavy, fat, bulky

Elysian- beautiful or creative; peaceful and perfect

Alexithymia- the inability to express your feelings

Frisson- a shiver of pleasure

~AN: waiting for a smog on Grams. I love my car. But update update updated!

Hope you enjoy!
~~~~~~~~~~~~~~~~~~~~~~~~~~~~~

20

C hapter 20

"Come here." His voice was soft as he waved her over.

Haley stood next to Xavier with her hands folded in front of her. He pulled her down to his lap with a light 'umph' as he no longer envied the air for he was wrapped securely around her as if a caterpillar was cocooned before turned into a butterfly. He now sighed with content as he took a big breath in with his nose on Haley's neck. He let his warm breath fan her as frisson ran down her spine.

Haley had instinctively curled and molded her body to the angles and curves of Xavier as she took in the warmth that radiated from him. In this moment it seemed to Haley like everything was perfect. Like the harsh past that the two mates had faced was whipped clean away and the future could be nothing less than excellent as they were each other's querencia all because the two were pulled to each other by a bond.

The mate bond.

Haley was yet to discover what it is but she felt that she could do anything if she was just belong side Xavier and no matter what they did physically it was fine for the girl who had experience nothing because she felt so comfortable and loved by her mate.

In this position the two stayed for what felt like an eternity but was really about twenty minutes. Within this time Xavier took in the presence of his mate and was choosing how to tell her that he will have to be leaving. He wondered if he should tell her everything or even invite her with him. Eventually he decided to speak up.

"Tomorrow, would you like to go visit Steven and Bethany and possibly spend the night there? Or would you like to come with me on a trip." He spoke slowly wanting Haley to understand the different options before she picked.

Haley put thought into this answer before she leaned forward to grab the pen resting on the desk and a piece of paper.

'I would prefer to stay with the Devin's.' She wrote neatly.

It was not that she didn't want to be with Xavier. It was the unsure change of scenery with different people who don't understand why she doesn't speak and so on.

The rest of the day was spent with the two mates in Xavier's office. That night Xavier made sure that Haley had a bag of clothes to spend the night there as they had took what she owned on their last visit.

That night the two fell into a calm peaceful sleep that brought a longing into Xavier's heart as he knew the next day and possibly the one after that he would hardly see his mate and get to spend virtual no time together.

*

Xavier woke up early getting himself ready before he woke his mate up.

Haley had woken to a hand caressing her cheek softly as if she was a delicate vase that could break in an instant. When she opened her eyes she was met with the very structured face of Xavier who was wearing a long sleeve navy blue button down tucked into charcoal gray pleated slacks that sported a black leather belt around his waist.

When she heard a deep chuckle her head snapped up to the handsome face of her mate who was still chuckling with a sly smile. That's when Haley knew she had got caught not just staring but admiring the fine man in front of her.

A deep red blush spread like a forest fire over the pale cheeks of Haley embarrassed with how blunt she was with her attraction towards Xavier. She knew what mates were and that Xavier was hers but she was still shy and new to the subject to find it okay to be so blunt with her actions.

"It's okay amor. I enjoy when you stare. You understand the feelings I have towards you too." Xavier voice laced with his wolfs which made it huskier as desire for his mate filled him.

Haley who had tucked her head in the pillow when caught pulled it out now looking back to her mate. With her prominent blush now fading she gave a light nod and Xavier spoke again.

"We have to get you to the Devin's. Let's get up." With another nod Haley got up.

Moving around the room to get ready it didn't take her long which was quite disappointing for Xavier as he enjoyed watching everything little move that Haley had made. When she was ready she turned to him oblivious to his stare.

Xavier stood with Haley's bag in one hand and her hand in his other. He moves swiftly through the halls into the garage where he opened the car door for Haley and shut it once she was in.

Xavier walked around and got in starting the car. He reversed until he was out of the grave and started the drive through the woods and onto "city streets" as it was really homes every hundred acres or so.

Haley kept herself occupied by watching the passing trees and twiddling her thumbs till Xavier large hand captured both of her smaller ones. It definitely caught Haley by surprise but she was okay with it for she very much enjoyed the tingles and warmth that spread by just his hand. Her fingers now played with Xavier's as they twist and curled around each other. It was not till they were more than halfway there that Haley had let their hands rest in the last position which was interlocked with her other hand covering the outside of Xavier's. They stayed like this till they pulled up to the Devin's home.

They both got out of the car and Xavier pulled out Haley's bag meeting her at the front step as she knocked.

Bethany had opened the door and pulled Haley into a hug kissing the top of her head. She then pulled Xavier in taking the bag and setting by the stairs.

"Steven told me everything. Take your time. Well take care of her while your gone." Bethany said rubbing Haley's back as the two girls faced Xavier.

"Thank you for doing this." Xavier nodded ready to leave.

Haley ran to grab a paper from the kitchen and came back. She used her hand as a table as she wrote quickly.

'Where are you going?' She wrote never thinking of asking till now.

"No where important deliciae." (Darling)

'When will you be back?' A feeling of alexithymia ran through Haley when she thought of Xavier leaving.

It was soon replaced when monophobia washed over Haley even though she knew she would be staying with the Devin's while he was gone.

"I'll be home within two days amor dulcis." (Sweet love)

Xavier pulled his mate in for a hug as Haley buried her face into his chest breathing in his familiar scent as if it was the last time she ever would. Xavier planted a kiss on the crown of Haley's head. She looked up and their eyes meet.

"Num occidere me tu diligere. Simul cum eo non poterit redibo neglegis." Xavier spoke as if he was struggling because internally him and his wolf were both having a hard time leaving their mate.(Love you are killing me. I'll be back soon because I can not stand being away from you)

Xavier kissed Haley's forehead and turned to walk out of the door. Once he left Haley felt kind of empty, She missed him immensely, and a need for him washed over her.

Little did Haley know Xavier felt the same exact way.

~~~~~~~~~~~~~~~~~~~~~~~~~~~~querencia- a place from with ones strength is drawn

alexithymia- an inability to express ones feelings or emotions

monophobia- a fear of being alone

~AN: next chapter up!

Enjoy!
~~~~~~~~~~~~~~~~~~~~~~~~~~~~

21

C hapter 21

Haley ate very little dinner that night with the Devin's. The mates were all talking gaily about their day and admiring each other as Haley felt mopey and out of place with them. It was unusual for her to feel that way with Tyson and Bethany but she just thought she missed her mate and that was the problem.

Which actually was true because Xavier felt mopey too but knew he needed answers or anything at all to try and keep his Haley safe.

Haley decided she should just shower and go to bed as there was nothing better to do and she didn't want to stay with the couples.

Haley found it comparatively difficult to actually fall asleep though which was not like her at all as she loved sleep and her body usually craved it with her lack of nutrients.

The problem was her body craved the touch of Xavier more and more as more distant was put between them. It was as if Haley and Xavier had a string connecting them and the further they got from each other the further that string pulled wanting them to snap back together.

A frustrated huff came from Haley's lightly parted lips as she sat up in bed. It had been three hours of trying to fall asleep but her mind only wandered back to Xavier and stayed wide awake.

She stood from her bed wrapping the fluffy brown comforter around her slim body as she walked to her window seat. The same window that Xavier had took her from. She rested her forehead against the cool window pane looking out into the dark forest she loved to explore and then she closed her eyes. Within the next forty five minutes she was asleep with her face pressed against the glass of the window unattractively.

This was not the case for Xavier. He knew he would get no sleep so he traveled all day through Colorado and up to North Central Wisconsin where the Moonstone pack is located. It was about a twenty hour drive and if he drove through the night he could make it there at about nine in the morning. He would not have to stop and try to sleep because he knew he wouldn't be able to without his mate in his arms. Not only would he not be with his mate but he wouldn't be getting information about his mate quick enough if he decided to stop.

*

Making it to the border of the Moonstone pack at nine fourteen Xavier was quickly let through and directed to the Alphas home. Getting there quickly he stepped out of the car to be greeted by the Alpha, Beta, and Delta.

Perfect. He though as now he wouldn't have to go looking for the person he needed. The older man was standing right in front of him.

"Alpha Daron. How may we help you." The Alpha spoke getting straight to business.

"I would like to speak to your Delta, Steve. I have some questions about your granddaughter, my mate." Xavier said addressing the Delta who looked taken back for a moment.

"Yes of course. Come. I'll call my wife as well." The Delta answered accommodating Xavier.

Xavier followed the man into the house as he was lead into a open white living room.

"Please take a seat. Flora should be here shortly." He spoke about his wife as the men took a seat opposite of each other.

An older lady walked in with a lovely smile of her face as she saw her mate. Xavier then caught her eye.

"Hello. I am Flora." She greeted the Alpha confidently.

"Hello Flora. I am Alpha Xavier. Haley's mate." He replied loving the way he could openly call Haley his mate.

Then the conversation started to flow. The grandparents asked about Haley and how she was. If she had figured out she was a wolf. As conversation continued it was now a deeper topic about Haley's mother and father.

Steve and Flora did not like to talk about who Haley's father was because they did not enjoy seeing Hadlee's mate turn on her. They thought it was terrible, no one deserved to have that happen, and that wolf didn't deserve a mate to begin with. They were also not the biggest fan of Jake taking cared of Haley instead of Alpha Gunner but we're glad that Haley had a loving father and Hadlee a loving husband.

They explained how Hadlee had only been with Gunner so he was the biological father but he should have no clue that Haley was even born. They also explained how Jake took care of her as his own.

After the explanation the mates started to get curious.

"May we know why you need this information Alpha Daron." Steve asked kindly.

"Please call me Xavier." He started as the ranks didn't matter now that they should be considered family to some degree. "We have got a couple of messages about Haley's "real father" wanting her and possibly hurting her. All Haley knew was her father was dead so we didn't understand. Now it makes sense as Alpha Gunner has been trying to contact me more often. Thank you for the explanation."

"They want to attack her?" Flora said taking in the new information.

"I don't know. I'm guessing so at this point but I didn't have enough information on who and I still don't understand why." Xavier spoke thoughtfully about his mate that he adored.

That was almost the exact same thing Haley was thinking about that night. Xavier, how she adore him and think of him as hers. He said they were soulmates after all. She knew these feelings were not ones of just liking someone and not ones of loving a family member. She almost felt as if she was just infatuated with Xavier as that was what she constantly thought about.

Him.

She wondered what he was doing. What he was thinking about. Where he was. If he was okay. If he was happy. If he missed her as much as she was missing him.

Her mind continued to play a slideshow of pictures of the two as she was drifting off to sleep. Some things had already happened other things didn't and she wished they had. One was her sitting on Xavier's lap in his office while another was her on his lap in their bed kissing. She had never been kissed but it was as if she could feel his firm but soft lips on hers and the arm that started to tightly wrap around her waist. It was warm and safe.

Until it wasn't.

22

- -

C hapter 22

Haley's mind continued to play a slideshow of pictures of her and Xavier as she was drifting off to sleep. Some things had already happened while other things didn't, but she wished they had. One was her sitting on Xavier's lap in his office while another was her facing him on his lap in their bed kissing. She had never been kissed, even by Xavier, or any guy for that matter, but it was as if she could feel his firm but smooth lips on hers and the arm that started to tightly wrap around her waist. It was warm and safe.

Until it wasn't.

His lips on hers were no longer warm and inviting but cold, rough, and cutting off her oxygen supply. His thick bulky arms were not safe but now crushing and digging into her bony sides.

The picture of Xavier in her mind started to become fuzzy or blurry and start to fade away as the pain became numbing and it all vanished into nothing but black.

*

Xavier was now on his way back. He stayed to have lunch with his mates grandparents, the Alpha, Beta, and their mates. It was silent as almost all the people were slightly intimidated by Xavier dark and muscled appearance but that didn't mater to him as it always happened no mater where he went.

In what little conversation was held the Alpha offered any of his assistant to Xavier who may possibly need or want it as the Moonstone pack was not very far from the Full moon pack that was ran by Alpha Gunner. Besides Haley was born here. Once family, always family. It was just the same for her mother Hadlee, she always had a place in the pack.

Xavier gave his thanks and appreciation to everyone there before and as he was leaving. It shocked the older Alpha as Xavier was always look at as if he was uncaring and ruthless, not thankful for anything, but it was about his mate. Mates change everything.

The drive seemed unbearably long as he just wanted to be home with his mate, his Haley. Xavier had over a fifteen hour drive left when he started to think about Haley. He wondered what she was doing at that moment in time. Maybe she was thinking about him. He also thought about being with her and got excited. He couldn't wait to have her wrapped up in his thick stump like arms, holding her as if she was the most delicate work of pottery, and cherishing her as if she was the most important ancient artifacts in his lineage.

A smile began to spread on his love intoxicated face as thoughts of his large hand exploring Haley's ink black curled strands as his lips caress her flushed cheek roaming down to meet her jaw and then to her neck. He imagined her straddling his lap and pulling him close as he preformed those actions. She would stroke the back of his neck as whimpers of pleasure coursed through her filling the room until she took his earlobe sweetly between her lips grazing her teeth over the doughy flap of tissue. She let it go and her warm breath washed over the side of his face and two words followed.

"Mark me." The sweet voice pleaded.

Xavier was pulled from though when he realized he was going well over one hundred miles per hour. A deep shaky breath was released and he shook his head to get rid of any other thoughts, but one.

Is that what her voice sounds like?

Xavier ignored all thoughts by turning on the radio. It's not that he had it off because he disliked it he just never had a lot of time to listen to it as he has more important things to take care of.

*

When Xavier finally got back into White River he was excited but tired. He had been awake for over forty hours but that did not stop him from speeding to the Devin's home at four o'clock in the morning. It almost encouraged him more as he was ready to fall asleep with his mate.

The streets were dark and empty as Xavier took all the turns to get to his mate. He thought he would have felt her more as they had been separated and now are coming closer but he ignored it and thought he was to enthusiastic to notice.

He pulled into the driveway cutting off the engine. He got out of the car hopping to smell the sweet but light smell of citrus and flowers but it seemed faded and not as strong as he expected. Walking up to the front door his fist flew rapidly against the solid wood door.

Steven came down the stairs to open the door. He didn't say anything as he opened the door enough for Xavier to walk in expecting him to go straight to his mate.

Which was exactly what he tried to do.

He nodded to Steven as he walked in the house and started up the staircase remembering where his mate slept. Into the hall Xavier expected to be flooded with Haley's familiar scent but was disappointed when it was only slight stronger than outside. He turned the handle to the door and lightly pushed open guessing Haley would be asleep.

And she was asleep.

Just not him her room like Xavier expected. As well as Steven, Bethany, Tyson, and Natalie who had no clue why they were getting woken up by a terrifying angry Xavier.

23

C hapter 23

Haley was woken up by her body feeling light in the air until she hit the ground with a flat thud. A grown ripped through her lips as Haley never remembered being in this much pain. A cynical laugh was heard over Haley's grown.

"You think you can hide from me? I know things about you that you don't even know about yourself. You will not carry my blood line for you are a measly little girl, you are not trained to run a pack. You would never be fit just like your mother and that's why I picked my own Luna. She's the strongest woman of all and produced a well bred heir to my reign. I will have my son slaughter you, you worthless pup!" The croaking scratchy voice yelled at the half conscious Haley who couldn't focus on a word he said.

The heavy door thundered as it was slammed shut cutting off any light to the dingy, vulgar smelling room.

Haley silently thanked anything that was listening as she was great full for the yelling to stop and the light diminishing. Those factors only added to the pounding of her skull.

On the other side of the tick medal door Alpha Gunner stomped down the dark floors stained crimson and the foul smelling halls that lead to the dungeon entrance.

"I don't want to hear anything from Haley! If I hear as much as a peep from that small rat I want her tortured! Like I should have done to her worthless mother, that pathetic mate of mine!" Gunner spoke angrily to the head guard that took care of anything and everything in the cells.

The guard named Shane bowed his head and quickly rushed out a 'yes Alpha' before Alpha Gunner strolled off to find his son.

The day went by and Haley had took several naps through the day because she couldn't even move due to the pain. All she wanted was Xavier. She had hoped, wished, and prayed to everything she could think of that she would soon be reunited with her mate.

Haley had never noticed till now that she quite enjoyed his scent but now she missed it as it was long gone and not there to comfort her like Xavier's bed or his neck. Haley longed to nuzzle her nose into his neck that greeted her with warmth and tingles while holding her favorite scent. It even passed up her Orange Blossom shampoo or the smell of Bethany's potatoes and bacon.

A sigh of pain flew from her lips.

A sigh of relief came from the lips of the head guard Shane as he walked into his home greeted by the smell of his favorite food, spaghetti and meatballs. His wife Denise made the best food in his opinion. She always claimed that it was easy and her brothers mate Lindsay made the same exact ones when they ate but Shane still though his wife's were better.

"How was your day honey?" Denise asked her mate as he wrapped his arms around her waist while she finished cooking the noodles.

"Alpha Douche-hole threw a girl named Haley in the cells today. She was so skinny and small she looks like she could be maybe thirteen. He said to tortured her if she made so much as a noise. All she did was lightly groan when she woke up. I think she's related to him somehow though. He said her mother was his mate and he should have tortured her too. I don't even understand." Shane explained utterly confused about the whole situation that went down with his hated Alpha this afternoon.

"Hm I feel like I know that name. Maybe I'll think of it. Well I'm sorry. I hope she doesn't end up hurt. Alpha Gunner went crazy after Hadlee left. Remember the first trip togeth- OH MY GOD IT'S HADLEE'S DAUGHTER!!! HALEY!" Denise finally realizes that she knew the girl in the dungeon cells and knew that she immediately needed to take action to get her role model's daughter to safety.

Denise knew what Alpha Gunner was planning and she knew that he would follow threw if not stopped. His own son didn't even want to follow his fathers footsteps but he was forced to.

"We need to get her out of there. We will keep her here if need be but she can't be killed. She was the girl at the birthday party on the first trip." She whispered to Shane

He instantly pull back with wide eyes knowing exactly who she was and what she meant to his mate. That meant she basically means the same for Shane. Besides this was his chance to prove the Alpha wrong.

"We take her tonight. There's a teen guard on the shift. We can go through the back. She will stay in Destiny's room. It's the highest one and with all the perfumes she has it will mask any scent. We need to let the kids know about this though." Shane replied already having a plan.

"Kids it's time for dinner!" Denise yelled as their oldest daughter at nine came bounding down the stairs with their twin boy who were seven, Leo and Levi tumbling down behind her.

The two mates informed the kids on what was going on, how it was to work out, and that NOBODY under any circumstance was to know about what was happening.

The kids rushed to nod and set everything up to help their parents.

Leo and Levi shared a room that night while Destiny waited for her parents to come home with the girl. She was waiting to hear the front door close and lock so she could turn on the bath. There was a delightful concoction that she made with all her favorite most scented flowers. With Lilac, Daphne, Jasmine, Gardenia, and Honeysuckles the bath would bubble and blend perfectly.

She had got clothes from get mothers and fathers closet as well as her own to make sure that Haley would have what fit her most and she was most comfortable in without the worry about asking for anything.

24

- -

C hapter 24

The door closed and locked. There were two sets of footsteps coming up the stairs which Destiny though was odd but she started the bath anyways. The bathroom door opened and Shane was carrying the thinning, chicken skinned Haley.

"Take care of her." He whispered to Destiny kissing the top of her head before he walked out.

Denise walked in and stood in front of the shaking figure of Haley. She reached her hand out to touch her shoulder in a nurturing way but Haley still flinched.

"Dear, it's me. Denise. Your mothers friend. I came to your ninth birthday party. I'm here to help you...This is my daughter. Would you like to get in the bath?" Denise asked slowly in a small voice to keep from frightening Haley.

Haley slightly nodded tugging at the hem of her blood and dirt covered clothes.

"I'll help you undress and we'll get you in the bath." Denise explained as she started to lift the shirt over Haley's head as if it were a mother and a child.

Destiny offered her hand to the now naked Haley. She helped her step into the bath as she observed her body. Haley was grossly skinny and bruises covered much of the pale skin. As she finally stepped in Destiny turned the water off.

"Do you want anything yet? Or would you like to wait till after the bath?" Denise asked waiting for a reply.

Haley just shook her head which confused Denise but Destiny somehow understood.

"She doesn't talk mom. And if she did she would be in shock. Wait till after she's out. Maybe pull up notes on my IPad. She can type what she wants to say then. It's on my desk." She spoke with intellect as she was showing her mother that she was mature and could handle bigger problems then most at her age.

"I'm Destiny. Let's wet your hair and get you clean okay?" She almost whispered to Haley as she was down on her knees ready to assist bathing Haley.

Haley slightly nodded for the second time since she was rescued from that prison. Destiny took that as the okay to start getting the blood out of Haley's curly hair. She lightly massaged in her favorite strawberry shampoo into the wet hair and did the same with the conditioner after. Pouring a generous amount of her vanilla bean body wash into the sponge she placed it in Haley's hand.

"Can you hand me the brush mom? She has curly hair and it's all matted. We can only brush it out now with conditioner." She spoke and her mother beamed, proud of her for taking on the responsibility of bathing another person who wasn't a baby and really thinking about everything while doing so.

After the bath Haley took Shane's jacket and the yoga pants that Destiny had put out. They walked into Destiny's room and the IPad was already sitting in the middle of the bed with notes pulled up like Destiny had asked.

The three sat down as Denise handed the device to Haley and started to ask questions.

"Are you okay?"

'Yes.'

"Do you remember me?"

'A little bit.'

"Do you know where you are?"

'No.'

"Do you know how you got here?"

'Not really.'

"Do you need anything. Can we do anything for you?"

'I wanna go home.' With Xavier she thought.

"Where's home?"

'Colorado. White River.' Denise gasped quietly while Destiny's eyes widened but for different reasons.

Destiny though Haley was really far from home. Denise thought what if she knew or was in Alpha Daron's pack. Alpha Gunner though he was big and bad but everyone was more afraid of Xavier than Gunner, part of why Gunner wanted to take Haley.

"Who do you stay with?" Denise asked lightly knowing that Haley no longer had her mother or Jake who Haley thought was her father.

'Xavier. He's my mate. I want him.'

"Alpha Xavier Daron?"

Haley only nodded in reply as there was no need to type a reply. She wasn't completely sure about the Alpha part but knew his last name started with a D.

"Okay darling. We will try to contact him tomorrow. Is there anything else you need tonight before we go to sleep?" Denise asked looking at the clock that said one forty eight A.M.

Haley shook her head no again as the two stood up from the queen size bed.

"Okay get some sleep. No need to wake up in the morning at any time. The kids will be home around one in the afternoon and I should be here at three. The last to get home is my mate, Shane. I'll leave a note on the counter if we leave before your up and you need anything. Okay?" Denise explained the whole routine to Haley who nodded taking in the information.

The two left the room as Haley got under the sheets. She wished she was wrapped up in Xavier's arms. She knew soon she would be able to thanks to Denise and her family for taking care of her and possibly getting her home soon.

25

C hapter 25

Xavier groaned as the phone rang blearing obnoxiously causing his pounding headache to feel like an explosion in his skull. He had been up for over two days and did not plan on actually sleeping till he found his mate and she was safe in his arms. The phone continued to ring as he looked up from the territory map of Wisconsin that was sitting in his desk in front of him.

With a deep breath in Xavier picked up the phone trying not to scream at the person on the other line about how he's busy and needs to find his mate.

"Hello? Alpha Xavier Daron?" A feminine voice that he did not recognize asked.

"Yes." Was his only reply and Denise felt overwhelmed with joy as she could reunite the mates.

"This is Denise from Alpha Gunner's pack. I have your mate Haley. I want to get her back to you as soon as possible. I knew her mother so I only want to help her, I promise." Xavier didn't know what to say as he was relieved and wanted to yell in joy from the emotions he was feeling.

"I can go to the farthest south west boarder with my mate and possibly sneak her through but we have to do it soon or Alpha Gunner will know she's out of the cells." Denise broke the silence.

Xavier let out the breath he was holding in since he heard that someone has his mate.

"I'll be there tomorrow by noon." He spoke quickly knowing he needed to go and if he left now he would make it by then.

But what if this was a trap. What if she wasn't helping Haley but just luring Xavier in to quite possibly kill him.

That didn't matter now or even if that were to happen. Xavier needed his mate to be okay and keep her safe even if that meant himself dying.

Xavier mind linked his Beta. Reid immediately knew he would have to take charge of the pack for the time being again. After he did that he quickly ran to the garage getting in his car and pulling away.

The only think on his mind was getting his mate as he drove completely past the speed limit not caring. He needed to make the twenty hour drive in less than eighteen hours plus the time change between the states making it more like sixteen hours.

*

They called Xavier and Haley was ecstatic. She not only missed being away from her mater for over three days when it was originally not even supposed to be one and a half days.

Denise had told Haley right after the phone call that Xavier would be at the boarder of the pack by twelve o'clock noon. She also explained how both her husband Shane and herself would take her to the boarder to deliver her to Xavier.

Denise knew this was risky and that if Alpha Dickwad found out that Haley was gone before they could get her to Xavier all hell may break lose and someone would definitely get hurt but it didn't matter at this point. All that mattered was Haley get back to her mate, Denise and Shane's family stays safe and knows to ALWAYS do the right thing even if the Alpha disagrees.

*

Haley hardly slept at all that night as she was just ready to be back In Xavier's arms where she felt safe with the tingles that shot through her body. She always wanted to giggle or gasp at those feelings as it tickled and always seemed to take her by surprise.

Haley was exhausted by the time she got up at ten forty three in the morning. Her body required much more sleep than she was actually given the last two days and her body still hurt from getting beat and thrown into a prison cell. She was thankful that Destiny had a pair of jeans that were to big for her, Denise had shoes that were to small for her, and Shane had a pull over hoodie.

After Haley threw on the clothes that they had got out for her she headed down stairs and was greeted by Denise and Destiny cleaning the house while the two boys were playing in the living room.

As Haley walked in the Kitchen Denise turned around to greeted the sickly looking girl with a warm motherly smile.

"Do you want something to eat?" Denise asked Haley who only shook her head no as she wasn't hungry, she was past that point.

Haley found a marker and a note pad on the fridge. She pulled it down and sat down at the table to write.

'Thank you guys for everything you have done for me even if the last time you saw me was when I was nine. It means a lot that you guys would do all this.' Haley wrote feeling emotional about what a old friend of her mothers would go out of her way to help her get back to her mate.

"It's really no problem. I'm actually really glad I got to see you again. It would be really nice to catch up under different circumstances." Denise opened her arms to hug the long lost friend.

Haley gladly excepted the hug that made her feel like family. Denise felt like she could have been Haley's older sister or even Aunt with how Jake and Hadlee had always treated her.

26

- -

C hapter 26

Haley gladly excepted the hug that made her feel like family. Denise felt like she could have been Haley's older sister or even Aunt with how Jake and Hadlee treated her.

"We need to leave now! Alpha Gunner is walking to the cells. I know it's early but it's our only chance." Shane barged in rushing to get his mate and Haley out of the house.

"Mom can I go with you guys?" Destiny asked quickly for she's really liked Haley even if she didn't talk she felt completely comfortable with her.

"Baby you can't come. We need to get her safe and Alpha Gunner can't find out. Alpha Xavier may think we're a threat. We can't have you getting hurt." Denise rushed out getting ready to make a break for the door.

Haley hugged Destiny as a 'thank you' and sent her a half smile. Destiny sent a sad smile back but already had a plan. She would just follow behind to see Haley off.

After about a minute Destiny stepped outside and followed the scent of her parents that was lingering in the air. As she run after them she got a new smell. She knew it but couldn't place from where. She followed till four people came into sight.

The fourth person wasn't supposed to be there. It was Alpha Gunner.

Destiny mind linked her mother and father immediately.

'Alpha Gunner is behind you!' She yelled to her parents.

'Damn it Destiny I said stay home!' Denise yelled upset with her daughter disobeying.

'Guards are coming and fast. We have to shift. Destiny keep running till your out of the territory with Haley. Her mate should be here.' Shane ordered as he and Denise shifted to fight off the guards and Alpha.

Destiny sidestepped so she was out of the way when her father pounced onto the Alpha. Haley had stopped running unsure of what to do or where to go. Destiny grabbed her hand and started running again.

"I'm gonna shift. You need to hold on tight okay?" Destiny yelled as her pulled them behind a tree.

Shifting into a light brown medium sized wolf Haley's eyes got big. Destiny didn't care that her clothes were ruined she only cared about the safety of her new friend. Haley slowly got on unsure.

Once on Destiny took off making her way to the boarder much quicker than she would have on foot. She ran past territory line not thinking about anything and everything out there.

Destiny knew there was a road if she continued but she knew she would have to speed it up when a menacing growled ripped through the air right behind her. She could feel the hot breath of another wolf on the very end of her tail. Destiny growled knowing if she dodged through trees she could possibly lose this guy.

Running faster in and out of trees, taking hard turns until Destiny saw a tall man running at them. Haley squeezed Destiny's fur between her fingers tightly as Xavier darted towards them.

Xavier was excited until he saw a big wolf behind his mate that was chasing her and the wolf she was on. He let out a thunderous growl that boomed through the forest.

"Run straight, there is a car. Get in till I come." Xavier yelled at Destiny and Haley as he ran and shifted in front of them to fight the wolf.

Haley looked back in shock. When her eyes followed the giant black wolf he raised his paw and sliced through the throat of the other. Haley winced and buried her face into the fur of Destiny.

Destiny slid to a stop right in front of the car that Xavier was talking about. Haley got off Destiny and opened the door. Destiny shifted and quickly got in trying to hide her naked body. Haley got in after and locked the doors.

Haley just sat there shell shocked. These people she knows and loves turn into big giant dogs.

After a while Xavier came running back in a pair of basketball shorts with scratches all over his chest. He knocked on the door softly bringing Haley out of though. Destiny was curled into a ball asleep as she had never ran that fast or hard or with the extra weight in her life.

Haley unlocked the doors and Xavier opened it with urgency to hold his mate in his arms. The tingles shot through both of them and Haley sighed as she missed the feeling. She missed the warmth and safety of Xavier's stump like arms. She missed the natural smell of Xavier and he missed and her smell too.

They pulled away and Haley kissed Xavier's cheek. He rested his forehead on hers and breathed in deeply looking into her eyes. Destiny shifted in her sleep and the two pulled back completely.

Haley pointed to her and then tugged on her own sweater asking Xavier if he had anything to cover Destiny.

"Let me look." He spoke softly opened the back hatch.

He looked for clothes but only came up with a blanket.

"Is this okay?" He asked showing Haley.

She nodded taking it from him and covered the small frame. Haley also buckled her into her seat and moved to sit in the front. Xavier walked around to the drivers side and got in.

After complete silence for a couple of minutes Haley tapped the hand of Xavier who was just resting on the gear shift. He looked over to her and saw her point and Destiny in the backseat.

"She's coming to our pack. Her family will come soon as well. They don't want to lead the pack which would be mine but I don't need land out here. They would be next to lead as they help kill Gunner but they don't want to take over. So his son the next rightful Alpha will lead as you are my Luna. They don't want to be looked at as traders so they will move to our pack... I know it's a lot to take in but you can ask any questions when we get home Okay?" Xavier explained as he put his hand on the knee of Haley cris crossed legs.

She nodded understandably and then intertwined her fingers with Xavier's. She blushed profusely as he looked over and squeezed her hand. Xavier smiled to himself as he was driving home.

"Rest amor meus speciosus." Xavier spoke softly as he could tell Haley was tired. (My beautiful love)

Xavier couldn't wait to get home. Not for food or to take a shower, or even just the sake of being home, but to hold his mate in his arms as he falls asleep with her scent surrounded him like a cocoon. He sighed at the though and continued to speed down the road with his hand in his mates.

27

C hapter 27

Haley woke up with a yawn and a stretch. She was still in the car with Xavier's hand on her lap but this time she knew exactly where she was. They were driving down the forest surrounded road before they would get into the long driveway of Home. Well Xavier's home, but that didn't matter because they lived there together and wherever Xavier was Haley felt safe enough to call him home.

They pulled in the driveway and Haley turned to wake up Destiny. Lightly shaking her arm her eyes groggily opened as she rubbed them.

Haley pointed to the house and got out of the car waiting for Destiny to get out. When she did she first fixed her blanket and then took Haley's outstretched hand. Xavier smiled as he held the door open for the two still sleepy women.

Haley lead Destiny into a room just down the hall from Xavier and her room. Haley pointed to the bathroom and then tugged on her jacket. She walked out pulling the door closed as Destiny walked into the bathroom.

Haley got some clothes from her closet and walked back into Destiny's room setting them down on the bed while the shower ran in the bathroom.

When she walked back into her room she wanted to take a shower but got distracted when she saw Xavier laying on the bed. Haley took off her shoes and pants, getting comfortable and crawled into her mates arms. He took one long whiff of her hair and pulled back a little.

"You don't smell the same." He states not enjoying her full natural smell.

She shrugged her shoulders lightly looking up with a slim smile spreading into her face. Xavier chuckled and Haley dug her head into his bare chest. She kissed lightly on his upper chest. That lead to delicate kisses sprinkled across his chest, shoulders, neck, and collarbones.

As Haley did that Xavier thought of how she took care of the little girl that was two rooms down. Yes Haley had road on her trying to escape a wolf but they had got in the car and Haley wanted something to cover her. When she woke her up it was soft and motherly, just like the way she held out her hand to lead the girl into her room and brought her clothes without even a conversation. Xavier liked watching his mate take care of people, she would make a great Luna. The pack would just have to adapt to her not talking which would be new. As Xavier though more about it she would make a great mother, of his pups.

Xavier pulled Haley's face away from his chest and pulled her to his face with a light grip. Now that they were face to face Xavier examined everything centimeters of Haley's face as if she was the most beautiful work of art he had ever seen and he wanted to memorize everything about it.

Haley felt slightly uncomfortable under Xavier tough gaze but looked into the beautiful brown eyes of her mate. She loved the different flecks of light brown around the midnight black pupil. A delicate sigh came from Haley's pale lips. It was one of content and relief.

That surprised Xavier as he had never heard an audible sigh from her lips.

Before Xavier knew it he was leaning in to kiss his mate. He started to get excited as Haley leaned in as well with her eyes fluttering closed. Haley's soft lips delicately rested on Xavier's and instantaneously warmth, passion, and need spread through both their bodies.

The mates simultaneously pulled back from the kiss. Xavier opened his eyes waiting for any type of response from his mate. When Haley's eyes fluttered open the biggest smile spread across her face and she had never felt like this in her life.

It shocked not only Xavier but Haley also as sutterted words flowed around the room in a sweet light voice.

"I lov-ve y-ou." Haley spoke just higher then a whisper.

Xavier was stunned frozen with eyes as wide as saucers. His mate had the most angelic voice he had heard in all his life. It was so soft and smooth even with the stutter.

Haley blushed as red as a rose as her body heat up. She had confessed deep feelings for her first words to her mate and she got nothing in reply.

"Sss-sorrry." She whispered turning away.

A tear leaked from her eye and she felt as if a giant whole was caved into her chest actually bringing her physical pain.

Xavier felt her saddened emotions and it brought him out of his shocked state.

"No amica mea, te amo nimis. You have the sweetest voice of an angel." Xavier rushed quickly. (My darling, I love you too.)

Xavier pulled Haley into his lap. Her feverish body pushed against his as her back was smashed onto his chest. Xavier tucked his chin into her pink neck leaving soft chase kisses over her traps and a even softer one on the spot when he was patiently waiting to mark her. The softest moan floated through the air and stoped at the ears of Xavier.

"M-may I take a-a show-wer?" Haley asked looking straight forward.

Her sad emotions and pain was gone but it was replaced by a tingling ache in her core that made her want to squirm and tightly cross one leg over the other when Xavier spoke and touched her. She had no clue it was arousal in her core but the sweet hot smell gave Xavier that clue.

"Only if I may come with you." Xavier voice growled as it was filled with lust.

Haley didn't know what came over her body but her actions took her into motion without a thought about it. She feverishly nodded her head and stood taking the large hand of Xavier's into her smaller one. She pulled him up and walked them into the bathroom.

~AN: two more chapters!!!!

Hope you enjoy!

28

- -

C hapter 28

"Only if I may come with you." Xavier voice growled as it was filled with lust.

Haley didn't know what came over her body but her actions took her into motion without a thought about it. She feverishly nodded her head and stood taking the large hand of Xavier's into her smaller one. She pulled him up and walked them into the bathroom.

Xavier inspected Haley as she pulled the jacket over her head leaving her only in panties. Xavier grew hard by looking at her and his pants became to tight and constricting. Haley felt self-conscious but also beautiful as Xavier stare at her. Her panties stuck to the wetness of her lips as she pulled them down.

With the little confidence that Haley had she turned to Xavier completely nude. She took two small steps towards him and pulled up on the hem of his shirt getting him to help take it off as he was to tall for Haley to do it by herself. Haley then squatted down to come face to face with the large bulge showing through Xavier's pants. Haley looked up to Xavier as he put her hand on the button to make sure it was okay. When he nodded she undid the button and zipper pulling his pants down slightly and then hooking a finger in the waistband of his boxers taking then to the grown together.

Haley stood up and turned to the shower and turned on the water stepping in. Xavier cautiously followed her actions until he wrapped his arms around her small waist. As the water warmed they stepped under together letting it cascade around their bodies. Xavier got the soap gently lathering up Haley's body.

The moments they shared in the shower together were not all that sexual even with the pull of need between the two. It brought them closer together in a comfort with each other's body where there was a knowledge that they both held about every inch of the others body. No limit were pushed or boundaries exceeded.

There was love in every action that they preformed and there was a connection made without words.

Haley still had questions for Xavier and so did Xavier along with just wanting to hear his mates voice, but both knew this was not the time to ask those questions as they both somehow had the unspoken conversation of it being after the shower when they were just laying together in bed.

Haley enjoyed the shower. Xavier did too as he got to reach another level of intimacy with his mate that he hadn't before, but it was different for Haley. It was excepting of how she did not speak for the last year and it was not pressuring her to open up in anyway uncomfortable.

Xavier reached around the small frame of Haley and turned off the water. He stepped out and offered a towel to Haley. As they got dried off they walked into the closet. Xavier pulled on boxers and Haley slipped on her panties. She walked over beside Xavier and pulled a shirt off of the hanger.

A smile slid across Xavier's face as he not only enjoyed seeing his mate in his clothes but she felt comfortable enough to do so.

As they walked out of the closet they walked to the bed and got in. Xavier sat with his back resting against the headboard and his legs out straight. Haley lay perpendicular to him with her head on his lap wet curls sprawled over his leg and the bed and her feet just dangling off the side of the bed.

Haley examined from the firm defined chest to the bulky shoulders and arms. Even if you were to double possibly even triple Haley's size she would still be hidden behind the mass that is her mate.

"So you t-turn into a wo-wolf?" Haley broke the silence testing new words that hadn't been used in a while.

"Yes. I'm a werewolf. Everyone around here is. Even yourself, you just can't shift or haven't yet." Xavier answered nodding his head.

There was quite a pause as this was new for Haley but she seemed to be taking it will.

"We are mates because we were picked to be with each other." Xavier added on.

"My mm-mom a-and da-ad are too?" Haley's voice quivered with thought of her parents it wasn't a stutter this time.

"Well your actual father was the one who took you. Your mom ran away from him even though they were mates. He tried to hurt the people she loved so she ran back home where your dad, Jake was. He took care of you like his very own daughter.

All of them were werewolves, even the Devin's are. Tyson runs his pack as the Alpha, just like me." Xavier finally looked down after he spoke.

One lone tear slid down Haley's cheek as she missed her mom and dad. She wished she could have had them meet Xavier.

"No, don't cry amor" Xavier whipped the tear pulling her into his chest.

"I miss them." Haley whispered.

"They were why you stopped talking?" Xavier asked coming to that conclusion while Haley only nodded.

Xavier continued to comfort Haley till she was ready to speak again.

"Why can't I turn into a wolf?"

"We can go find out later but you might have just not shifted yet."

"What's a pack?"

"Wolves like to stay in packs. It's like one big family where they protect each other. They have a leader the Alpha which I am. You are the Alpha female or my Luna because you are my mate. Reid is my Beta which is the second in charge. He takes over when I'm gone."

"Al-pha." Haley quite tested the word that sent a thrill through Xavier. "Alpha."

"Yes, and I should introduce you to all the people in my pack."

"Okay. When?" Haley spoke ready for what she thought to be a big next step.

"I would prefer after I mark you. There are men without mates who would want you but you are mine!" Xavier spoke with a rising volume and Haley felt the need to calm him down.

"I am yours. You can mark me." She pecked his lips and cradled her head in his neck as she spoke.

"I think we should wait a while. Once I mark you we would want to complete the mating process or if we wait you would go into heat."

"What's that?"

"The mating process would be for us to...make love. And heat is when your body gets hot and it's painful and only I would be able to take it away." Xavier looked for better words than just sex so Haley wouldn't become to embarrassed.

"How?"

"The same thing." This is when Haley blushed and hid her face in Xavier's neck as she was now straddling his waist.

"We will wait until you want to do that love." Xavier spoke stroking her damp hair kissing the exposed part of her neck.

As he continued to kiss he hit where he would mark her. A moan escaped her lips as she wanted more of the pleasurable sensation. The kiss led from her neck to their lips that kissed sloppily with a want burning inside both of them. Xavier's hand roamed Haley's body as the other was stuck in her hair. She opened her mouth wanting more and thinking of this being the only way.

They pulled back for a breath and Xavier day dream from days before flashed through his mind. Haley kissed down Xavier's jaw as he didn't go back to kissing her once they caught their breath. From his neck and to his lips Haley kissed till she pulled back.

"Mark me." Haley spoke with confidence in a demand.

And Xavier followed her orders.

29

C hapter 29

Epilogue

Haley was dressed in a beautiful white gown that flowed elegantly down her straight frame. Denise was down on the floor helping Haley into the jeweled foot thong. Laura was in front of Haley applying a tad bit of makeup. Destiny and Bethany were working together to pulled her messy curly hair back into the perfect hairstyle. Natalie was fixing everything with Haley's dress.

The off the shoulder dress showed off the mark that had magnificently healed from Xavier. That was the main point of this dress, to show off his mark. They pulled her hair back into a low neat but messy bun to show it off even more as there would be no hair in the way to cover the pink skin. Haley loved the mark, from the way it looked on her neck above her collarbone, to the heat that sparked in her when Xavier kissed it.

Haley sighed in content and opened her eyes to see a beautiful dressed up version of herself. She had on eyeliner to make her eye pop with a little pink lipstick so her lips weren't as pale as always.

The dress that hung off her shoulders was an ivory color. It took a dip at the middle of Haley's chest to show off her slightly swollen breasts. Down the back button lined the middle from her shoulder blades down to the floor as her dress dragged behind her. The women helped Haley stand from the chair.

At that exact time Xavier knocked on the door waiting for his mate. He waited no more than a few seconds as Laura opened the door.

"She's ready!" A giant smile slid on her face waiting for the reaction that Haley would get from Xavier.

Laura opened the door more and Haley stepped into the doorframe shyly. As she stepped forward and came into view of Xavier his eyes darkened to almost a black as lust filled his body.

"MINE!" The thundering growl shook the house as Xavier took his claimed mate into his arms and kissed his mark on her.

Haley looked over she's shoulder and smiled.

"Thank you guys." She thanked the women and they smiles as a your welcome and walked out of the room.

"I want that dress kept on and nothing messed up mister!" Bethany spoke to Xavier walking out of the room behind the rest of the ladies.

"We're all yours." Haley whispered softly kissing Xavier ear.

Xavier kissed his mark and then pulled back. His lips softly brushed Haley's and she connected them. Smiling into the kiss Haley started to chuckle. Xavier pulled back with a wide smile.

He stepped back and got down on one knee in front of her.

Leaning forward he gave Haley's slightly protruding belly a kiss.

"I can't wait to meet you." Xavier spoke in the softest voice Haley had ever heard talking to their growing fetus.

"We should get going my Luna." Xavier stood up taking Haley's hand.

She blushed lightly and nodded not sure if she was really ready to be a Luna.

They walked down the stairs hand in hand. Once outside Xavier lead them up to a stage. They stood off to the side till Beta Reid introduced Xavier.

Haley looked out over the ocean of people standing in front of her. They looked at Xavier and her with adoring eyes. Some were sniffing the air.

"Hello ladies and gentleman. We are gathered together today to officially meet my mate and our Luna." Xavier deep voiced boomed but his eyes smiled with love for the women next to him.

The crowd roared and cheered in acceptance of their Luna and with joy that they finally have one.

Xavier made Haley repeat a small oath to the pack as their Luna. Once she finished she stepped back. She felt like she except something into her body that slightly weighted it down but made her feel ecstatic and pleased.

"Hello Luna."

"Your so lovely."

"My Luna."

Many people spoke and she looked out to the crowed to see them all bowing and no one saying a word.

"It's your mind link with each of the pack members. Like the one we have." Xavier reminded Haley. "It means they expect you as their Luna."

As Haley was reminded she put up the block to stop people from communicating with her at this moment. She would later take it down but she wanted to take everything in and adjust a little at a time.

"You have marked her! Does she yet bare your pups Alpha!?" The excited question was screamed from the crowed.

Haley blushed and cradled her face into Xavier's bicep.

"Your Luna bares my mark and our first pup." Xavier informed the crowed who went into an uproar.

After the ceremony and party Haley sat in Xavier's lap as his hand rested on her stomach. They sat around with the Devin's, Xavier's Beta and Denise's family just casually talking.

Tyson's mate Natalie was pregnant with their first child and couldn't wait to have more. Laura had a son with Reid who would be the next Beta. Haley had just found out she was pregnant two days ago when she and Xavier went to the doctors to see if Haley would ever shift.

Haley was for sure a werewolf as she immediately connected to a mind link when Xavier marked her but they wanted to know more. At the doctors they ran a few test and said Haley's wolf is most likely dormant or dead as she would have been a late shifter and then experienced such trauma with her parents dying. When they ran the test they found Haley to be pregnant as well.

It didn't shock the mates as much as it surprised them as they had only had sex two times. Haley was unsure if she was ready as she had never planned to have kids much less at the young age of nineteen but Xavier was more than ready. He had wanted to be a father for the majority of his life and even more after his father had died saving him from a rouge attack at a young age.

Haley felt ready after they talked about it when they got home.

"I love you my Luna." Xavier spoke lowly and kissed down Haley's neck.

"I love you too my Alpha." Haley replied lovingly kissing Xavier's lips and they looked into each other's eyes lovingly.

And they lived happily together with their son Alexander.